Trust Your Heart

Emily Hussey

Book 2 in the Red Centre Series

Note that Australian English is used in this book. Spellings will be different to standard spelling used in the United States. Some of the terminology may be unfamiliar to readers outside of Australia.

Copyright © 2018 Emily Hussey
ISBN 978-0-6482972-1-5

Editor: Lauren Clarke
Cover Design: Getcovers
Cover Images: Depositphotos

Published by Winsome Books 2018
Second Edition 2023

A division of Winsome Enterprises Pty Ltd
Adelaide, South Australia

Contents

Also by Emily Hussey 4
Chapter 1 1
Chapter 2..15
Chapter 3..26
Chapter 4..36
Chapter 5..51
Chapter 6..61
Chapter 7..81
Chapter 8..98
Chapter 9..112
Chapter 10..122
Chapter 11..130
Chapter 12..143
Chapter 13..153
Chapter 14..164
Chapter 15..178
Chapter 16..198
Chapter 17..205
Chapter 18..221
The Red Centre Series 231
Emily Hussey..232

Also by Emily Hussey

The Red Centre Series
Journey to the Heart (*Prequel*)
The Red Heart
Trust Your Heart
Follow Your Heart

Stand-alone Titles
Ambition and Passion
Maison Angelique

Harrow Series
Wild Spirit (*Prequel*)
Wild Destiny
Wild Tempest
Wild Fire

Sandy Bay Series
Secrets at Sandy Bay
Escape to Sandy Bay
Return to Sandy Bay

Writing as Rowena Wylde
Plan B: Secret Donor Baby

Chapter 1

NO SHOES, NO service. Sarah winced as she slipped her shoes back on. Teetering on the killer heels, she picked her way around the tables and revellers in the beer garden. They'd seemed a good idea when she'd planned her outfit. The sliding doors to the bar area were pushed wide open allowing the music to spill out over the lawn area beyond.

Hot and sweaty bodies pressed against each other in the confined space. Sarah pushed through the crowd and fronted the bar. The blanket of stuffy, oppressive air inside threatened to suffocate. How could people stand it? That was why she felt unsteady, and not because of the night's champagne. Staff were run off their feet trying to serve the crowd. She leaned against the counter to take the weight off her feet. *Don't make me wait too long.*

"Like a seat?"

Sarah turned to look at the speaker. The man beside her slid off the bar stool on which he perched and offered it to her.

"Thanks, but I'll be fine. I'll be served soon."

"I've been here for a while and the barman rarely makes it down this end of the room. You should make yourself comfortable."

The stool looked inviting. Her feet screamed, "Take it! Take it!"

Sarah eyed the seat. Glancing up, she found herself looking into eyes of brilliant blue beneath jet black hair. It was an attractive combination. The man had a touch of silver grey on either side of his temple, adding an intriguingly distinguished look to his appearance.

He gave her a small smile, and she dropped her gaze. *He knows I was checking him out.* A flush rose over her neckline towards her face. She'd forgotten how to flirt if that's what he thought she was doing. She was out of practice with a lot of things.

"It's warm in here, isn't it?" the man said. "The heat's getting to me too." This was delivered with a wry smile as he mopped at his face with a handkerchief. "C'mon, take the weight off your feet."

That did it. "Thanks." Sarah slid onto the stool. Her feet had priority over any concerns she might have. Anyway, elevated her to a better height. The barman could see her more easily.

"So," he said, "do you come here often?"

Oh God, is he going to be a creep? If that's the case, I'll get off this stool and move up the other end of the bar. I'll probably get served quicker up there anyway. She looked at him again, and those smiling blue eyes. No, he was just being corny. Anyway, the view was better at this end. She rolled her eyes obligingly.

"Sometimes. It's a popular watering hole. We usually drop in at the end of the week."

"We?" The raised eyebrows slid up into that interesting hairline.

"I work for StationAir, so mainly the air crew, mechanics and a few hangers on. Industry people. I haven't seen you here

2

before." That didn't sound too much like an interrogation, did it?

"That's because I'm new in town. I arrived last week to take over management of the local radio station. I'm Joel, by the way." He extended his hand.

"And I'm Sarah." The formality surprised her, but she took his hand anyway, noting his firm handshake and smooth skin. From the corner of her eye, she spied the barman moving in their direction. She leaned forward to catch his attention.

"Scuse me!" a voice beside her called out. "The lady here wants to buy a drink!"

"Yeah, her and a dozen others," muttered the barman but he stopped in front of her. "Yes love, what'll it be?"

"I'll have three Drambuies, one with a dash of cream."

The barman pulled a bottle down from the top shelf and busied himself with finding the liqueur glasses. Sarah stole a quick glance at her neighbour, who was staring into his own drink. He had an interesting profile—strong jaw and aquiline nose. What was so absorbing about that drink? Was he thinking of his next corny line?

She flicked away to watch the barman's progress, not wanting to be too obvious in her interest. She could play the casual game too.

"So where do you fit in? Are you part of the air crew or the ground crew?"

His voice was well-modulated. Perhaps he had voice training with the work he did.

"My feet are on the ground. I'm the office manager. I manage administration and work alongside the operations manager. I get into the air when I can—when the office isn't so busy or if there's an unusual flight available."

She kept her eye on the barman as she spoke, watching his progress. "Sometimes I tag along on a mail run. I like catching up with all the station people. It helps to put a face to a name when I'm processing orders and liaising with them by phone, etc."

"Sounds interesting. Different to being stuck in a recording studio. I want to introduce local colour to the programs so perhaps I can arrange interviews with the air crew. I could send a reporter out on a flight with you guys. Would that be possible, do you think?"

Sarah shrugged. "It would be up to the boss."

The barman came back with the drinks. The deep golden liquid with a creamy cap looked delicious. She could smell the honey flavour. She paid and gathered the small glasses together, careful not to spill a precious drop.

She slid off the stool, pleased she could stand upright with the drinks intact. That feat in itself gave her a surge of confidence.

"Why don't you join us? You can meet some of the others. We're out in the beer garden."

"Won't I be intruding?"

"Not at all. The more the merrier and you'll get to know some of the locals."

Sarah tried to sound nonchalant. She liked the idea of this stranger joining them. It was so long since she'd met anyone new and besides, it would introduce him to some more people. She could consider it a form of community service.

"OK… if you're sure no-one will mind?"

"Why should they? Follow me."

Sarah wove her way back around the tables, dodging the dancers and pausing at the doorway to check his progress. He was reassuringly close. She took deliberate steps on the spongy grass, hoping her shoes wouldn't make her unsteady. She would spill the drinks if she went sprawling.

She indicated the wedding group with a nod of her head. "That's us—the rowdy mob over there."

They occupied four tables, with people moving between them as they mingled or danced.

"Oka-a-ay," he said, "you mix with a remarkably well-dressed group of people. Rather flash. I might be under-dressed."

He wore jeans and checked shirt – typical Territory wear. Sarah briefly noted the snug fit of his jeans with the thought that it all looked fine to her.

"We've all been to a wedding. Kathy, a colleague married a local station owner today."

They arrived at the table where Mark and Chris were sitting, chatting with a couple of others.

"Mark, Chris—this is Joel. He's new in town and was sitting on his own at the bar so I brought him over to meet everyone."

Two sets of eyes looked up in thinly disguised surprise. Sarah flushed again for some inexplicable reason. What was it with her tonight? Must have been all that champagne at the reception. She carefully lowered the glasses to the table.

"G'day Joel," said Mark. "Pull up a pew. How long are you staying in Alice?"

Joel did as asked and fleshed out the detail he'd given Sarah at the bar. He'd drifted into radio work after leaving uni, cutting his teeth on the midnight to dawn shift and working his way up to a more desirable time slot.

"So, you're going to do the breakfast show or something like that?" asked Chris.

He took a mouthful of the beer he'd brought with him and shook his head.

"I leave that to others these days. After a while, I came out from behind the microphone. I enjoyed it but wanted to learn more. I took on some management roles to get exposure to all aspects of the business. This is the first time I've managed a station." He gave them a wry look. "I'm looking forward to both the challenges and the new learning experience. I think there are going to be plenty."

Mark and Chris laughed knowingly.

"So what about you two—what do you do?"

Chris answered for them both. "Choppers, mate. We fly 'em. Station work mostly but also some rescue work or whatever's going."

"Yum," muttered Sarah. "I haven't tried Drambuie with cream before, but this is absolutely de-lish. Great suggestion, Mark!"

"I can see that," said Chris. "The moustache suits you."

"The trouble is," she continued, while doing a great job of licking the cream off, "the glass is so small you finish it in no time and the cream makes the Drambuie just slide down. It takes so long to get served at the bar!"

"Well, you'll have to get two next time and then it will last you longer. Allow me. Anyone else for another drink?" Joel rose from his seat.

"Oh no, really," Sarah began, "you can't do that." She paused.

"It's no trouble."

"Well OK, but only one. That'll be more than enough."

"Mark? Chris? Can I get you another?"

"Yeah, why not? The night is yet young." Mark was in a convivial mood.

Chris shook his head. "I'll sit this one out, mate. It's time to pace myself."

Joel collected the empty glasses "I won't be long. The crowd is thinning out."

While he was away, Sarah was up and dancing with one of the mechanics. She had her second wind and the DJ played her favourite tracks. It had been a memorable night. She flung herself back into the seat as Joel returned.

"I really enjoy dancing. It's great to get moving, even though it's on the grass." She giggled at some of the gyrations other dancers displayed before picking up her liqueur and sipping appreciatively.

"Joel, you could become my best friend if you keep bringing me drinks like this. That creamy honey taste is divine." She took another sip. "It's smooth and mellow." Then it was gone, and she felt as mellow as the drink.

She beamed at the men sitting with her. "Mm—I can feel that tingling all the way to the tips of my toes."

The tingling was so good she wanted to dance again. Dare she ask Joel? She thought about it but was unexpectedly shy. She hardly knew him. What if he said no? She turned back to her friends. "C'mon Chris, come 'n' dance."

"Sure you're up to it, Sugar Plum? You've been on the go all night."

"I've told you before—don't call me that! Of course I wanna dance. C'mon!"

Giving a wiggle and a shimmy in front of him, she pulled him up and into the throng of dancers, letting the music and the rhythm take over. After his initial hesitation, Chris got into the swing of things, just not as energetically. The next track was a slow number.

"Thank goodness for that," he said. "I could do with something more sedate—it's been a long night."

He pulled her close into a slow, swaying shuffle. She settled comfortably into his arms, resting her head on his shoulder. It was nice to have a more relaxed pace.

"Hey, you're not a bad dancer you know," she mumbled.

"You're not so bad yourself." There was a moment's silence except for the music in the background. Sarah could see Rosie carrying a tray full of drinks towards others in their party.

Chris took a deep breath. "Sarah, I was wondering if you would like to...

There was a sudden smash of broken glass on the paving. Rosie had connected with the elbow of an energetic dancer. Broken glass and foaming beer frothed around her.

"Oh no! Rosie don't move; you'll step in all the glass. Chris, I don't have my shoes on. Can you help her?"

"Sure." He sounded a little abrupt. That wasn't like Chris. Getting tired perhaps?

Sarah retreated to a safe distance and directed the clean-up proceedings. That was her forte anyway. By the time the glass was picked up, the DJ was taking a break and she and Chris re-joined the others at the table where Mark and Joel were having an animated discussion about cricket.

Cricket! Why would people want to talk about that? Sarah made a point of seating herself beside Joel, wondering as she did what it was Chris had been about to ask. If it was important, he would raise it again.

"Well, I guess cricket makes a change from aviation," she remarked, "Personally, I find it as interesting as watching paint dry."

"Maybe that's because you don't understand the finer points of the game," Joel explained patiently while Mark rolled his eyes. "Next time there's a test match on, you'll have to watch it with me and I'll explain what it's all about. Then you'll see it differently."

"Oh, that would be... it would be... very interesting," she fibbed.

Chris and Mark burst out laughing but Sarah refused to look at them. She was not going to let an opportunity pass to sound a little engaged at the suggestion. She hoped she would never actually have to sit through a game. It was fortunate she was sitting down as she felt a bit flushed. *It's warmer than I thought.*

"Have you seen much of the town?" she queried, diverting the conversation to a safer topic. "Have you found a place to live?"

"I've been busy at the station since I arrived, so I haven't had time for exploring. I'm staying in this hotel, but only while the outgoing station manager packs up and vacates the company apartment. I'm moving into that tomorrow."

"Do you need any help?" Did that sound too eager?

"Thanks, but it's under control. The cleaners have been through and the apartment comes furnished. I only need to move myself in with my meagre belongings. I didn't bring a lot with me, so it won't take long."

He regarded her speculatively, a slight smile tugging at the corners of his lips. "I might be up for some afternoon tea, after I've hung up the shirts and laid out the toothbrush. Is that an option?"

"Maybe." She looked down at her bare toes splayed out on the grass to shield her eyes and her delight at the suggestion. She ignored the wordless exchange she caught shared by Chris and Mark. What she did had nothing to do with them. They couldn't protect her forever.

Looking up again, Sarah found herself looking straight into those absorbing blue eyes. They delivered an electrifying jolt. The gaze rendered her transparent, as though Joel could see the impact he was having on her. *What the hell? It's been so long since I've let myself enjoy any male attention. There's no harm in being friendly.*

"Hey, what about one for the road? The bar's shutting down soon and we'll all be turfed out. Any takers?"

Mark groaned. "I don't know, Sugar Plum. It's past the witching hour. It might be time to make tracks."

"Don't be such a party pooper! You can't skip out on me now. Just one more teeny-weeny drink?" she pleaded.

"I might have a soft drink."

"I'll join you," said Chris "but only a light ale. I'll get it, Sugar. It must be my shout. Joel, what about you?"

"I don't have far to go home so I can keep the lady company. I'll try the Drambuie but skip the cream. One white moustache at the table is enough."

Chris returned quickly with their order. Sarah sipped her golden liqueur, licking her lips with delight. She felt very mellow yet in a state of anticipation. It was a night of possibilities.

"It's been a great evening, hasn't it? Kathy and Alex are so well suited. Kathy might find some aspects of station life a bit of a challenge but I'm sure they'll be happy together."

"She'll cope," answered Chris. "She's one of the most competent and resourceful women I've come across—not counting present company of course."

"Thanks. I was about to pull you up on that." She tossed down the last of her drink. A deliciously warm glow permeated her body and her emotions expanded. She looked over at Mark and Chris. "Have I told you guys how much I really love you? You're the best friends a girl could have."

Mark chuckled. "Sure, Sugar Plum, we know, and we love you too. You're not having any more to drink, are you? It's been rather a full-on night."

"Mm—it's been a lovely night. There are lovely people here in Alice, Joel." She patted his arm. "I can introduce you to them. I'm sure you'll like it here."

"Hey Curly, I don't think I've ever seen you tipsy before." Chris ruffled her hair playfully.

"Don't do that, and don't call me Curly. And who says I'm tipsy? You know I never drink much."

They smiled indulgently. It was true—she didn't usually, but she'd made up for it on this occasion.

"Well," said Joel, "I'm pleased you talked me into joining you. It's been good to connect with some new people. I've been too busy finding my feet to get out and about much. It's time I did, so I might take you up on your offer of tour guide—if you were serious of course."

Those blue eyes again. The little creases in the corners crinkled when he smiled. Looking into them, Sarah felt stirrings, which were quite unfamiliar. Her gaze slid down to those oh-so-kissable lips and now she really thought she would melt. Wasn't it too soon to have feelings like this? Flushed and confused, she tore her gaze away. What was he doing to her?

She glanced back. A smile played around the edges of those delectable lips as though he knew exactly what she was thinking. Did he have this effect on all women? He was so complacently self-assured that he must.

The amplified voice of the DJ broke through her reverie.

"Hey folks, it's time for a wrap. One more track and that's me done for the night. I hope you enjoyed the music and look forward to next time."

The sounds of a recent release filled the air.

"Oh, that's brilliant," Sarah cried. "I adore this song. Who wants to dance? Who'll dance with me?"

"I'm beat, Sugar Plum," said Mark.

"Yeah me too," agreed Chris.

What pikers! How could they not want to move to the rhythm of the beat? She didn't dare look at Joel; she wasn't going to give him a chance of turning her down.

"That's OK" she said. "I can dance on my own."

Before anyone could object, she stood on her chair and stepped onto the table. It swayed perilously, and one glass fell over and dropped onto the grass beneath. She began an enthusiastic gyration, totally lost in the moment and the music.

Mark burst out laughing. "I've never seen her like this before. Come down, Sugar—you'll fall off and hurt yourself."

"If the table doesn't collapse first," interjected Chris. He grabbed another glass as it vibrated towards the edge. "Hey

Sarah—I'll dance with you, but you've got to get down. That table's not meant for boogying!" He stood up and grabbed her hand. She beamed at him.

"Oh Chris—you're such a spoil sport. This is my own private dance platform. Pity there's not room up here for two."

As she leaned forward to step down onto the chair, the inevitable happened. The table tipped, and Sarah, the table, glasses and bottles all ended up in a tangled heap, flattening Chris in the process. Mark and Joel managed to leap out of the way.

"Hell's bells. Chris! Sarah! Are you OK?"

Mark moved to lift the table away, gingerly picking his way through bottles and glass. Joel momentarily froze before moving to help. Sarah had sustained a small cut to her knee and a massive bruise to her ego, but otherwise was only shaken. Chris had cushioned her fall. He copped some bruising from the edge of the table but was manfully dismissive.

The hotel bouncer came striding over. He was a large man, all brawn and muscle—not the sort of person anyone would deliberately annoy.

"Right you lot," he bellowed. "I'll not have drunken behaviour on my patch. Get up and get out!"

Sarah's lip quivered. She blinked rapidly, her breath catching in her throat. "Look, it's my fault. I didn't mean it to happen."

"I might have known. *Cherchez la femme.* If you guys want to fight over a woman, you do it away from this pub. You've trashed the joint. Now get out—all of you!" He gave Chris a shove towards the door. "Move it, mate."

"Hey steady on. You might want to check a few facts first." Joel raised a hand to halt the onslaught.

"Don't raise your hand to me—I've seen all I need to see. I should charge you all for the damage." He took hold of Joel's arm. "Out, I said!"

"Let. Go. Of. My. Arm." Joel's voice was steely and so were his eyes. He fixed the bouncer with a stare that could have slayed at twenty paces.

The bouncer's response was to lash out, grabbing at Joel's shirt and wrapping an arm around his neck. Joel countered with a punch to his solar plexus. He hooked his foot behind the man's knees. They collapsed into a writhing, grunting mass of limbs on the floor.

"Stop it—just stop it!" Sarah screamed. "Chris, Mark—do something."

They were already moving and leapt into the fray to pull the two apart and restrain the bouncer. A guest from the wedding party ran off to fetch the hotel manager, while others moved to help Chris and Mark. Joel was assisted up from the ground. He had a flushed face and his shirt was torn but other than that, he seemed to have survived the assault. He massaged his neck gingerly.

"That man's a brute." Sarah struggled not to dissolve into tears. "Are you hurt?"

"I'm fine"

"Are you sure? It looked frightening."

"Quite sure. I'm not hurt. Only my pride if anything. It would take more than a bozo like that to put me out of action."

"I'm so sorry—so really, really sorry," she said over and over. "This is my fault. How could I have been so stupid?"

A wave of nausea washed over her. She clutched at her stomach and made a dash for the ladies' room, where she proceeded to divest herself of a significant portion of her recent alcohol consumption. Second time round, it didn't taste so good. By the time she had rinsed out her mouth and composed herself, she felt utterly miserable.

The manager arrived as Sarah re-joined the group. The altercation was under control, but the bouncer was very, very angry.

"Rabble, boss," he spat. "Out of control and violent. This one here's the main offender". He nodded in Joel's direction.

"Please," pleaded Sarah, "it wasn't like that at all. This is all a big mistake. I can explain."

The manager's glance flicked over her. Sarah was conscious of her dishevelled state and his lip curled. The look was not one of admiration.

"The only mistake I can see," he said "is that you can't handle alcohol responsibly. If anything like this happens again, I'm calling the police. You're all out now and you're banned from these premises for a month. I don't want to see any of you back before then. As for you," he turned to look at Joel, "you can get out too. Pack your bags and leave. I won't have trouble-makers in my hotel."

Chapter 2

WITH ONLY PALE moonlight for illumination, Sarah scrabbled with the key at the door.

"It's so dark," she wailed. "I can't see a thing."

"Here, let me."

The key was removed from her grasp and a body manoeuvred itself between her and the invisible keyhole. She felt fleetingly annoyed at the arrogance, and then annoyed again when the key slid into the lock and the door swung open. Joel groped inside the door frame. His fingers found and flicked the switch. Nothing. The interior remained in darkness.

"Has anyone paid the bills lately?"

"Damn. The power has been disconnected already. Usually, State Energy isn't so efficient." She paced a couple of steps along the veranda and then back again. "Kathy's only just moved out; she was the bride today. I thought this would be a short-term solution for you. You can't stay here though—not without power."

"Look, I'll be fine. It should only be for one night. I'll be asleep before long and when I've got my eyes shut, I'm not looking at much anyway. If you point me in the direction of the bed, I'll manage the rest. I can sort myself out in the morning."

Sarah grasped the doorframe for support. The idea of bed was the most wonderful thing she'd heard in a while. She struggled to keep her thoughts in focus. "You'll want to take a shower though and be able to find your toothbrush." She chewed her lip. "You'd better come to my flat. It's next door. You'll have to sleep on the sofa, but at least you'll be able to see what you're doing."

"I'm in your hands, but are you sure it won't create any problems? Does the company mind you putting up strange men in corporate accommodation?"

"They don't interfere with my private life if that's what you mean. I'm working on the assumption that you don't have any nefarious intentions." Sarah flicked him a hooded glance. "If you do, speak up now and I'll leave you in Kathy's flat in the dark."

Joel burst out laughing. "I wouldn't be capable tonight. You'll have to trust me. I don't think you'll need to keep your bedroom door locked."

She flicked him another glance but kept her thoughts to herself. The idea of Joel in her bedroom held all sorts of possibilities but her tiredness verged on incoherence. That and the fact she felt decidedly second-hand made her decide the sooner she got into bed the better.

She kicked off her shoes as she came through the door, leaving them where they lay. The apartment was a bit messy, but she couldn't worry about that now. At least the lights worked.

Dragging a pillow and some bedding from the linen press, she flung them in Joel's direction. "There's the sofa. The bathroom's through that door." She pointed in the general direction of the bathroom." Make yourself at home. I'll see you in the morning."

With a quick detour past the bathroom, Sarah shut her bedroom door firmly behind her. Her clothes slid off as she lunged towards the bed. Sleep claimed her even as she sank onto the pillowed surface. Her thoughts were no longer on the man who had to arrange his lanky frame in search of comfort on a space that was too short.

Dragged reluctantly into wakefulness by an urgent need to use the bathroom, Sarah slid off the bed. She found her way to the door more through familiarity rather than visibility. Her eyes squinted against the morning light, reluctant to open. Kicking aside the clothes which lay where she had dropped them, she reached for the door handle. Her mouth felt like the pits and she desperately needed a drink of water. She was embarrassingly aware from the vile fur coating her teeth that she hadn't cleaned them the night before. *What a night. My God, why do I feel so disgusting?*

Opening the bedroom door, Sarah was partway through before becoming aware of two salient factors. Firstly, there was a strange man stretched out on her sofa and secondly, she was stark naked. Freezing for an instant, she shot back into her bedroom, now very much awake. Who was he, and what was he doing on her sofa? She groped for her dressing gown and after dragging her arms through the sleeves, belted it around her middle. Confused memories swirled through her head. First things first—the bathroom was a priority.

Cautiously, she opened the door again and peered out. The reclining figure didn't move. A shock of black hair was visible above the blanket and not much else. The sound of steady breathing indicated he was asleep.

Sarah scuttled across the room and into the bathroom. More memories of the previous evening presented themselves in a sort of photographic slide show. The wedding, dancing, Chris and Mark, the hotel, more dancing, chatting to someone and then it got a bit hazy. Was there a fight somewhere?

Couldn't be—she didn't get involved in fights. Why did her head feel so bad?

Ever the pragmatist, she decided that a toothbrush, a shower and a cup of tea would go some way towards putting her world to rights. In the process, she would sort out the man on the sofa and work out where he fitted into the scheme of things and her hazy memory.

He might be James, she thought. *No that's not right. Justin? I wonder, did he and I... did we...? No, if anything like that had happened, I would surely remember. After all, he's on the sofa and I was in my room, and that must mean something.*

When she emerged from the bathroom, the sofa was vacant, and the bedding was neatly folded at one end.

"I hope you don't mind. I helped myself to a cup of tea." The man raised his cup in morning salute. "Would it be okay if I had a shower? Then I'll get out of your hair."

He looked remarkably at home in her kitchen, though his bleary eyes reflected a lack of sleep. Either the sofa was not long enough or not comfortable enough.

Now she could observe him properly, Sarah could see his height would not have concertinaed easily on her sofa. Looking into those eyes, the blue contrasting with visibly red accents, more of the previous night came back to her. Her embarrassment level rose in keeping with the memories.

Joel... his name's Joel. How could I have forgotten that? How long's it been since I've had such a hunk of a man in my flat? And here I am in a scruffy old dressing gown and hair that has a mind of its own.

She realised Joel was looking at her, a bemused expression on his face and a question still in his eyes. Of course. The bathroom. He wanted to use the bathroom.

"Sure," she said with the brightest tone that she could manage. It sounded more like a husky squeak than the calm and controlled quality that she sought. She cleared her throat, pulled the belt of her bathrobe tighter and started again.

"I'll get you a towel. You're welcome to breakfast as well. There's cereal in the cupboard and bread, eggs, whatever in the fridge. I'll get dressed then sort it out."

"Thanks. A shower first, I think. I would have made you a cuppa as well, but I wasn't sure if you preferred tea or coffee."

"Umm tea, but that's fine. I'll make myself one after I get dressed." She passed him a clean towel from the linen press. "There should be plenty of hot water—it's solar."

Sarah gave him what she hoped would pass for a smile, before she turned and made herself walk sedately to the door of her bedroom. What she really wanted to do was bolt through, slam it shut and claim sanctuary. She closed the door quietly and leaned against it, eyes closed. She remembered enough of the previous evening now to increase the embarrassment factor ten-fold.

The wedding had been fabulous, no problems there, but it was after they hit the hotel that everything went downhill. Why on earth didn't Chris and Mark stop her? Didn't they care what she did? The trouble was, she knew they'd probably tried to apply the brakes and knowing her, she'd totally ignored them. The situation she found herself in was all her fault, no matter how hard she tried to convince herself it wasn't.

Slipping on a pair of jeans, Sarah topped them with a crisp white t-shirt. She dragged a brush roughly through her hair and clipped it back out of her eyes. Her hair, full of bounce and determined curls, was what the hairdresser termed 'unruly', usually before trying to sell her yet another taming product. Those curls had an indomitable personality. They drove her crazy, even if other people thought they were cute.

My eyes, my god my eyes! Glancing in the mirror, two red orbs revealed themselves, highlighted by the dark shadows beneath. Sarah found a bottle of soothing drops in a drawer and thoroughly irrigated each eye, hoping the swelling and irritation would soon disappear. Carefully, she patted eye cream into the delicate tissue surrounding them, and applied a light coating of mascara to her eyelashes. She didn't wear much make-up normally, but the mascara treatment made her feel more presentable.

She heard water running in the bathroom. She opened her bedroom door quietly and peered around it, in case her ears were deceiving her. They weren't. The sound of the shower became more obvious. A freshly-rinsed mug in the dish rack indicated Joel had finished his cuppa.

She flicked the switch of the electric jug and put out the makings of a strong cup of tea. Should she make her guest some breakfast? There wasn't much in the fridge, but then she hadn't been planning on company. She had been right about the eggs. She could scramble some and serve them with toast. Everyone liked scrambled eggs and there were none of the issues such as hard or soft boiled. Even better, they were quick to prepare.

By the time Joel emerged looking and smelling delectably clean and faintly like her lavender body wash, Sarah was placing two plates on the table, already laid with salt, pepper and condiments.

"I thought you'd like breakfast before leaving," she said. "You said you were moving into your new apartment today, so my guess is you don't have any food supplies. Would you like another cup of tea, or perhaps coffee now instead?"

"I didn't want to put you to any trouble, but you've been busy. Thanks, coffee would hit the spot." He hesitated until Sarah indicated where he should sit. Even seated at the table, his presence filled her small kitchen.

"Coffee won't be long," she said, popping more bread in the toaster.

"Thanks. I'm hungrier than I realised." He reached for the pepper. She hadn't noticed before, but his knuckles were swollen and bruised. Memories of the fight came flooding back.

"Ouch. That looks painful. Do you need something for those bruises? I've got some arnica ointment."

He examined the swelling, wincing slightly as he gently prodded the back of one hand with the other. "It will be stiff and uncomfortable for a while, but I'll live. It'll teach me not to get involved in fights."

"It's not a common occurrence then?"

"Bar brawls? Not really my style but I have a low tolerance for bullies. When I saw that gorilla pushing Chris around, I saw red." He grimaced again as he flexed his fingers. "Looking at these, I'm seeing red again. Be okay in a few days."

Sarah fetched the ointment anyway, placing it in on Joel's side of the table. After a while, he did rub some into his knuckles. He came across as placid but could obviously react when provoked. He was impetuous even. *Interesting*. She didn't condone fighting but was impressed he hadn't stood by while Chris got belted.

He tucked into the eggs, giving Sarah an opportunity to contemplate him further. He was not the rugged type who often propped up the bar in Alice. There was a modish cut to his hair and his clothes indicated a sense of style and taste. It was a nice change. She could see what had attracted her the night before.

He wasn't vividly handsome, but he had a wholesome appeal and a look that portrayed both intelligence and curiosity. Intriguing on all counts. He sported a tattoo on one arm in a black Celtic design. She hadn't expected that.

"This is so good." His breakfast was fast disappearing.

She gave a shy smile. "It goes a little way towards apologising for last night. I don't remember everything and some bits I don't think I want to remember. I know I contributed to events leading to you losing your room at the hotel."

"There was a bit of heat, but it'll settle down soon."

"Yes, but I caused it. That much I do recall—well falling off the table anyway. This is not such a big town and I would hate you to get the wrong reputation through no fault of your own."

He shrugged. "I can handle my reputation. Don't worry about it. My evenings have been quiet up until last night so at least it was a bit of a change." He looked her speculatively. "Do you think Chris and Mark meant it when they said they would take me up for a flight?"

"I'm sure they will, when they've got an interesting trip booked or one for which it's okay to take a passenger. Remind them about it when you see them again. It just depends on how it fits in with *your* work schedule."

"You're right. I'll have to hit the ground running and it will take me a while to learn the ins and outs of the station. I'm not sure about the rosters yet, but I might have to do a shift or two in front of the microphone. It's going to keep me busy."

They settled into a companionable silence, finishing the rest of their breakfast. *This is sort of cosy. Here I am, having breakfast on a Sunday morning with a gorgeous hunk of a man who spent the night in my flat.*

If only it was as good as it sounded. *Whatever chance I had with him, I probably destroyed at the hotel. What was I thinking?*

Joel placed his knife and fork together, wiping his lips on a paper napkin. "So, what about *your* standing with the hotel? Didn't you say last night that often you patronise the pub?"

"Yes, I mean no… well sometimes… "

22

He raised a bemused eyebrow. "Yes, no, maybe? Is this a hedging-your-bets sort of answer?"

Sarah could feel a blush rising again. He was going to think that she was such a soak. "What I mean is that I don't go to the hotel unless it is to meet up with colleagues or friends after work. It's not every day but more likely to happen on a Friday night, relaxing at the end of the week." She sat back in her chair, in a gesture of confidence that she didn't feel. "I don't think there'll be any ongoing problem—once the ban is over of course. The hotel management will probably forget about it after a day or so. It won't be the worst episode they've ever seen, especially in this town."

There were other hotels in Alice but she wasn't going to mention them. He looked at her, his smile stretching to his eyes. They didn't seem so bleary any more. Was he interested in her? Was it possible she hadn't ruined things between them after all?

"I'll get out of your hair. Thanks again for helping me out last night. I would've been sleeping in the car if it weren't for you. You're very kind."

"That was the least I could do after causing the trouble in the first place. I'm mortified—you'd think I'd know how to dance on a table by now without falling off!"

"Hmm—perhaps the amount of cream you had in your Drambuie has something to do with it."

"You know, you could be right. I'll leave the cream out next time." Sarah laughed and flicked a quick glance at him. "Although some things are hazy, I seem to recall we discussed afternoon tea later today. Is that still on?"

"Sure, I hadn't forgotten. It followed the discussion about showing me more of the town."

Good —all was not completely lost. "What time and where should I pick you up? We can discuss the itinerary once I get there."

"If we make it about two, I should be settled in and the bed made, luggage unpacked and so on. If you have a piece of paper, I'll write down the address. I'm happy to meet you anywhere."

I wonder why he mentioned making the bed? Sarah rustled up a piece of paper and a pen. "I haven't decided where we'll go yet. It's too early in the morning. Picking you up is fine. Write down your phone number too."

Watching him clamber into the SUV painted with the radio station's logos, Sarah thought how hard it would be to keep your whereabouts secret driving around in a car like that. One of the negatives of living in a small town was that everyone else seemed to know what you were doing, when and where. How long before news of her overnight guest became public?

As she turned to go back inside, she caught sight of Brian, Chief Pilot for StationAir and occupant of one of the other company units. He was hanging out his washing.

"Morning," he called cheerily, punctuated with a grin and a wink.

...and what you were doing last night and who you were doing it with, reflected Sarah as she nodded in response. There was nothing to tell—not that anyone would believe her. That was another problem with living in a small town.

"Morning Brian." She kept her voice light and breezy. "Fantastic wedding, wasn't it? They're so well suited, even if it took them a while to realise that."

Having met any need to be civil, she scuttled back inside her flat. She needed the security of her own space—somewhere she could contemplate recent events in privacy. She had surprised herself by reaching out to Joel. Not that he wasn't attractive, but it was out of character for her. Was it too soon to take this step? There weren't easy answers and as she told herself—-all she was doing was meeting Joel for afternoon tea. There was no harm in that. It was just being friendly.

Chapter 3

SARAH LOOKED AND felt considerably different when she cruised down Joel's street checking for the right house number. She had discarded the jeans and t-shirt for a crisp cotton dress in soft yellow, over-laid with a white leafy pattern. She teamed it with a white bolero and white espadrille shoes. It was the closest she was likely to get to casually sophisticated, especially with her mass of curls.

Sometimes, her hair portrayed a reddish glint, which created attractive highlights. She noticed in the rear-vision mirror it was glinting today—either that or she was still viewing the world through a red haze. She was trying to present an image that was controlled and well—mature. Not effervescent. Certainly not unrestrained. That was her hope as she knocked on Joel's door, at precisely five past two, just to show that she wasn't overly eager.

"Welcome to my new abode." He moved to one side, allowing her to enter. As she brushed past him, she noticed his scent—aftershave perhaps, but diluted enough not to be overwhelming. Nice. Sarah was gratified she'd made an effort with her outfit.

His apartment was pleasant, though nondescript as might be expected in corporate accommodation. The furniture was largely flat-pack style, and ironically seascape prints decorated the walls. Perhaps they were supposed to make you feel cool when the mercury climbed over forty degrees. The vase of flowers on the table was impressive.

Joel looked cool and refreshed. He might have grabbed a nap through the day as his bleary appearance had disappeared. He was now clean-shaven, and the pale blue chambray shirt, rolled up at the sleeves, emphasised the colour of his eyes perfectly. *Yum. He still looks tasty in the harsh light of day.*

"I've brought you a housewarming gift," she said, proffering a jar of homemade lemon butter. "Citrus does well in Alice and we have a fabulous lemon tree in our apartment complex. I made it myself; hope you like it."

"I'm sure I will. Thanks. A good cook as well as a fabulous dancer—a woman of many talents."

Sarah lowered her eyes in false modesty. "You haven't seen half of them yet," she demurred.

He lifted an eyebrow. "You intrigue me. I look forward to the discovery process."

He surveyed the benchtops in the kitchen. "I think I'm sorted here. Shopping done, everything put away, local amenities checked out so as far as that goes, I'm under control."

"Good. I thought we could take a picnic out to the Old Telegraph Station. There are shady sites down by the river. We'll see how we go for time after that, and I can either take you out to Stanley or Emily Gap in the MacDonnell Ranges or we can save that for another occasion."

"I'm in your hands. I haven't been on a picnic in years. What do we need to take?"

"Don't worry, I've got it sorted. There's a café on site so we can get a hot cup of coffee, but I've packed some cheeses and other bits and pieces to nibble on."

"Great. Why don't we go in my car? That leaves you free to direct and talk."

Sarah laughed. "Talking has never been a problem for me, but I'm happy to be chauffeured."

They transferred the picnic basket into Joel's car and she directed him to the Stuart Highway leading north out of the main part of the town. The Telegraph Station was established in 1872 and was an important relay centre in transmitting messages between Adelaide and Darwin. It was located close to a water hole, and the first white inhabitants of the area lived there, before developing the rest of the town in its current location. Now it was a reserve, picnic spot and historic museum.

Sarah relayed this information on the short drive to the Station. They found plenty of spaces in the carpark when Joel pulled in. The picnic area was close by.

"It must have seemed so remote when those first settlers arrived," said Joel. "They would have taken weeks to get here, by bullock dray I guess."

"Camel trains were used as well. I've often thought that those early men and women would have had no idea what was ahead of them when they left the city of Adelaide and headed north. Thank goodness for the invention of flight; that's all I can say." Sarah paused by a picnic table. "This looks okay— plenty of shade, and no ants."

Joel set the picnic basket on the table and they spread out the array of cheeses, olives and savoury bites Sarah had packed before taking a seat opposite each other. She sliced some cheese and balanced it on a biscuit, popping both into her mouth.

"Help yourself," she directed Joel. "I did think about putting in a chilled bottle of wine, but on reflection decided it wasn't a great idea."

"Perhaps not." His lips twitched. "Drambuie and cream might not be so good in the afternoon sun either."

Sarah stiffened. "I hope you don't think I'm some sort of lush. I know I overdid it last night, but it was the exception. It's not every day your best friend gets married."

"Hey, no need to explain. I was joking; it didn't mean anything." He patted her hand lightly. "Look, when you get to know me better you'll understand my sense of humour. You may put the lush in luscious, but I don't think you're any sort of alcoholic."

She removed her hand and placed it on her lap. "So, you think I'll get to know you better?" *Luscious? Is he reverting to corny again? Is this good or bad? Does he think now that I'm a pushover?*

He laughed. "I thought that was what we were doing, but I'm not in any hurry. I like to take my time over some things and savour the moment."

"Sounds like you're sucking a piece of chocolate—I'm not sure how I feel about that analogy." Sarah licked her fingers, before wiping them on a paper serviette and brushing the crumbs from her lips. "I know that you're here to manage the radio station, but what else is there to know about you? You inferred last night you're not an axe murderer but what deep dark secrets are you hiding your past?"

"What would you like to know? I'm an open book." He paused, head on one side for a moment before continuing. "I'm one of ten kids and we lived for the first few years of my life in a bus as my parents, who were products of the peace, love and happiness movement in the sixties, travelled the country getting work here and there. My mother was a classically trained pianist and gave concerts in local towns."

He piled some cheese onto a biscuit and bit into it, still managing to talk. "As we kids came along, we learnt to do some song and dance routines and sometimes joined our mother in a supporting act. Our father was a clockmaker, having done his apprenticeship in Switzerland and when we arrived in a town, he would repair all the clocks and watches needing an overhaul before they upped sticks and moved on."

"Wow! That was a different childhood. When did you stop travelling?" Her childhood was boring by comparison.

"After a few years my parents decided they'd gone as far as they wanted in the bus and sold it and bought a yacht instead. At that stage they were based in Fremantle. They took sailing lessons before heading off up the west coast of Australia. There were too many kids to fit on the yacht so the older ones went to boarding school and the younger kids were home schooled. Finally, they dropped anchor at Byron Bay on the east coast and have lived ever since on a property in the hinterland."

"What an amazing upbringing. Did you manage to make friends as you travelled? Do you still sing and dance? I hadn't picked you as an entertainer—beyond radio work I mean."

"Actually, the last thing I would ever subject you to is the spectacle of me singing and dancing." Joel grinned. "The look of amazement on your face is priceless. I'm sorry—I'm just teasing."

She folded her arms and sat back from the table. He'd been stringing her along. "Do I really look so gullible? No don't answer that. The obvious answer is 'Yes'. You had me totally sucked in."

He loaded another cracker biscuit with cheese, taking a bite before answering. "The reality is far more prosaic. My father is an engineer and my mother is a teacher. I grew up in a modest three-bedroom home in inner Melbourne, and my sister Carla is my one-and-only sibling. It's nowhere near as interesting as ten kids in a bus. I can't even begin to imagine what that would have been like—total chaos probably."

Sarah threw an olive at him. "I don't think I'll believe anything you say from now on." She folded her arms and sat back.

"Don't get mad at me," pleaded Joel. "When I was a kid I fantasized about that sort of scenario—-anything other than conventional suburbia. It was a variation on the idea of running away to join a circus. In reality, I went to the school at the end of our street and had to keep my head down because my mother was a teacher there." The face he pulled indicated this situation had not been to his liking. Who would like being in the same school as their mother?

"How did you end up in radio? Did you always want to do this sort of work?"

"No, not at all. I was accepted into engineering at Uni, following in Dad's footsteps but soon realized that it wasn't for me. Dropping out was my one mark of rebellion, and then I got the job at the radio station." He reached for the olives, pausing to survey the different varieties before making his selection.

"I'd done some voluntary work with the local community radio station and that gave me a leg up. Dad was disappointed, but accepted it was my decision."

"So—here you are in Alice Springs." Sarah observed Joel speculatively. She really had questions of a more personal nature. Had he ever been married; was there anybody special in his life, but she wasn't game to ask. It would be intrusive when she had only just met him.

Was he a good kisser?

That thought again? Her mind moved in uncontrollable directions. She reined it in. Time to move on.

"I'm more than ready for that cup of coffee, and then we can take a stroll along the river. There's not much in the way of water now but it's still a pleasant walk," she said.

They packed away the remains of their picnic and fronted the café. It did a roaring trade with Sunday visitors. Opting for the take-away versions, they turned towards the river bank and the grassy path that followed the meandering sandy bed. Here and there, pools of water indicated this was a waterway. The river bed was quite wide and shallow, but the tidemark of dead grasses and reeds by the edge showed that at times it became a raging torrent, sweeping whatever or whoever was in its path along with it.

"How are you bearing up after your late night?" Joel asked. "I only saw the end of it but from what I heard it seems that the evening was a blast from the very beginning."

"It was a wedding celebration so wasn't exactly a riotous event if that's what you were thinking. I haven't danced so much for ages, but the DJ played all the right tracks. It was fabulous except for the last bit—sorry about that—but it was good to see how happy Kathy and Alex were."

She gave a small sigh. "If I am honest though, I do feel rather second hand."

"You've bounced back remarkably well today. I'm impressed."

Sarah laughed. "A leisurely stroll is all I'm capable of. I'm glad I have time to recuperate before returning to work. A low stress day is just the antidote I need."

"Under the circumstances I appreciate you showing me around. I could have come out by myself, but it's much more enjoyable in the company of a local. I wouldn't have thought to come here if you hadn't suggested it."

Sarah flushed, ducking her head and letting her hair swing forward to hide her face. *Why do I do that,* she thought with exasperation. *I should have outgrown blushing years ago. It's so childish.* She looked up again and brushed her hair back. "My pleasure—the least I could do really. I didn't expect it to be so warm though." She glanced sideways at him to see if he was laughing at her. He wasn't. "I know you probably have preparations to make for tomorrow—settling into a new job and all that, but if you still have time, there's one more place I'd like to take you."

"I don't want a late night, but sure, I don't have to race back to the apartment just yet. Is it far?"

"It's closer to town. It's rather special. I think so anyway."

"Now you have me intrigued. Lead on."

When they were back in the car, Sarah directed him towards the centre of town. They didn't quite reach the main street however as she made him turn left and climb a steep road that wound its way up the side of a small hill, overlooking the town. They left the car in the carpark near the summit and climbed the stairs to the lookout area. Spread out below, the township was displayed in late afternoon glory.

"Wow! Great view." Joel stood, hands on hips, surveying the scene below. Sarah indicated the obelisk beside them.

"This is Anzac Hill and as you can see it's the location of the memorial to the townspeople who've participated in various war arenas, not just World War 1. I love coming up here. The view is tremendous. The town is spread out below in the foreground and in the distance, you can see the MacDonnell Ranges and Heavitree Gap. The Ranges embrace the town—that's how it seems to me anyway."

She turned to face him, gesturing skywards. "We're early today but towards sunset, you can see the most beautiful array of colours from up here. It's almost magical seeing those oranges, pinks and lilacs creeping across the sky. That's when the birds start up as well, signalling the end of day. I never get tired of it."

"Thanks for bringing me up here. I am honoured you've shared your special place."

They sat for a while in silence, absorbing the atmosphere and comfortable with just being.

"You know," Joel said, "I had some doubts about coming to Alice. It's such a long way from everywhere, and I was leaving people behind. I alternated between thinking it was a great opportunity and deciding I had rocks in my head. I think it will be okay though; I think it will be all right."

I wonder who he's left behind? Nobody too special I hope.

"I guess every new job presents the challenge of the unknown," she said. "The experience gained here should be rewarding though. You have to wear more hats than you would at a large radio station in the city."

"Yeah, I've noticed that. I'm not sure if I'm the station manager, the tea boy or the copy writer. It seems to be all three, and all at the same time. As you say, it's great experience and I'll know operations inside out by the time I've finished here."

"I'm sure you'll cope. Anyway, I don't know how you're feeling but I think it's time to call it a day." Sarah smiled brightly trying not to look as weary as she felt. "If you drop me back to my car, I'll leave you to your early night."

The light changed as Joel eased the car back down the hill. The ride back to his apartment was quiet, with both seemingly lost in thought. Or perhaps Joel was just as tired as she was.

"Thanks Joel," said Sarah awkwardly as she hesitated at the door of her car. "It's been a pleasant afternoon. I hope it made up for getting you thrown out of your hotel."

"No, thank *you*. It's been a day of surprises really from first thing in the morning and throughout the day." He dropped a light kiss on her cheek and stepped back from her car, allowing Sarah to climb inside.

She could feel the flush rising again. *Early morning? What did he mean? Surely, he hadn't seen her when she peeked out of the bedroom? He'd been asleep, hadn't he?*

There was no way she was going to ask him. Slamming the car into gear, she gave him a weak smile and made her departure as soon as she could. *Mortification*, she moaned to herself. *That's my middle name.*

Chapter 4

SARAH RAN INTO Joel once after the afternoon of the picnic, and even then it was only in passing. Sunday morning was usually shopping day. There were several supermarkets in town, but she had her favourite when considering variety of stock, rather than convenience. The fact that it was near Joel's apartment had nothing to do with it. It shouldn't have been a surprise to see him hovering over the fresh produce. Their conversation was brief.

"Don't touch those strawberries. They'll have been in the cold room for days. They won't have a skerrick of flavour."

Joel looked up from the punnets.

"Sarah! Do you come here often?" The comment was delivered with a grin and she made a show of rolling her eyes in response.

"I only need a couple of things," he said. "I wasn't sure about the strawberries. They must have travelled a long distance from the farm."

"So much of the available fruit has made that journey. How's the new job?"

Joel's wry look said it all. "It's been head-spinning with long days. I'm enjoying it—don't get me wrong—but there's a lot to get my head around. Some days I wonder if I ever will."

Sarah nodded sympathetically. "Give it time."

"I'm flying back to Melbourne shortly. I have to spend a week in head office, learning more about corporate issues, and I'll be able to sort out some family matters while I'm there. Two birds with one stone."

Her fleeting heart-jump at the unexpected meeting settled down. "Okay—enjoy your trip. I'll see you around."

There wasn't much else to say. It was almost an awkward meeting. What did she hope for anyway—that he would invite her on a hot date? Surely, she'd left those expectations behind in her teenage years. She resisted the temptation to look back as she continued down the aisle.

"Okay—spill. What have you been up to? What's this I hear about you and some tall, dark stranger creating havoc in the pub after the wedding?"

The two women were in one of the StationAir meeting rooms, with the door shut.

Sarah groaned. "Is nothing secret in this town? Whatever you've heard, Kathy, it wasn't anything like that." She screwed up her face with the effort of recalling him to mind. "Well Joel *is* tall and dark but there's no me and him and it was all a misunderstanding. Who told you anyway?"

"Just about everybody since we got off the plane. You, my friend, are hot gossip at the moment." Kathy grinned. "About time too. Your life has been chaste for too long."

"And it's still chaste, no matter what anyone might say."

"So—what are you doing about that?" She raised an eyebrow in interrogation. Kathy looked remarkably refreshed and as Sarah noted, wore a gorgeous outfit she must have purchased on holiday. She had just the right willowy figure to show it off. One would hardly think she had just flown halfway around the world and then across Australia. She ignored Kathy's question.

"Enough about me. What about New York? You look wonderful—married life is treating you well."

"We had a fabulous time and yes, marriage is treating me very well—or rather my husband is. I'm still not used to referring to Alex that way, but it was a honeymoon to remember. I took heaps of photos and when I'm organised I'll show you, but first I've got something for you." A package was offered, followed by a hug.

"Kathy, you shouldn't have! Your honeymoon was all about you, not buying presents. But then, you know me. I just *lurve* presents."

The small parcel was exquisitely wrapped in gold foil. It seemed too good to tear and Sarah carefully eased the tape and paper off to disclose the box underneath. She flipped the lid open. Inside was a charm bracelet, one that she had admired in a magazine once and pointed out to Kathy.

"You remembered!" The surprise delighted her.

"Sure did. You've been such a support Sarah, not just in the lead up to the wedding but ever since I arrived in Alice Springs. I wanted to get you something special."

"You didn't have to do that, but thank you!" Sarah enveloped her friend in a big hug. I've missed you. How long are you in town? I want to hear all about your trip."

"We're staying at the townhouse for a couple of nights. Alex has some things he needs to do in Alice, and then we'll head out to Mulga Downs. He'll drive and I'll take the station plane. Alex is letting me fly his precious Cessna 182."

Kathy was a pilot with StationAir and had met Alex, a station owner, in the course of her work. The two women had met when Kathy joined the flight crew, doing charter flights around Central Australia. Like many station owners, Alex had a pilot's licence as well and his own aircraft.

"We've decided to have a barbecue out on Mulga Downs next weekend, and everyone's invited. It's a sort of post-wedding thank you for all the support we were given in the lead-up to it and we can tell everyone about New York. You wouldn't believe what a big American city is like after living in Alice for a while."

By everyone, she no doubt meant the crew from StationAir, plus a few friends and neighbours from both in town and out bush.

"You'll come, won't you? What about Mr Tall, Dark and Handsome? You could bring him if you like."

"Absolutely, yes I'll come, but as for Mr Tall Dark and Handsome as you call him, no I couldn't. His name's Joel, by the way. It's not that sort of relationship." *Yet.*

"Give it time," replied her friend pragmatically. "It'll develop when you're both ready."

She ignored the exaggerated eye-roll Sarah sent in her direction.

"I've spoken to a few people but I'll contact the rest in the next couple of days. It will be an overnighter of course. You can have one of the guest rooms in the house. Others can stay in the staff quarters or bring their swags."

"Sounds like a great opportunity to catch up with everyone. Can I just ask that you don't provide any Drambuie and cream?"

Looking faintly puzzled, Kathy picked up her bag.

"There must be a story in there somewhere. I have to pick up some supplies now, and I need to see the wedding photographer, but I do want to have a proper catch-up before I head out to the station. Come to dinner with us tonight and you can fill me in on what's happened while I've been away."

"I thought you'd already heard what there was to know."

"Not quite everything. I want to hear it from the horse's mouth, including about the Drambuie."

❧

The morning after her conversation with Kathy, Sarah delivered some freight to the company hangar. It had to be delivered to stations the next day on the mail run. She enjoyed this aspect of her job. It got her out of the town office, and gave her the opportunity to catch up with airport-based colleagues.

"G'day Curly!"

"Colin—you're always one to cheer up my day. How's life in the hangar?"

Colin was the head mechanic, and always up for a chat. There wasn't much that happened in the tight airport community that he didn't know about. "It's all the better for seeing you, Curly."

She gave an exaggerated sigh, hands on hips. "How many times do I have to tell you not to call me that? You give everyone else ideas."

He threw back his head and chuckled. Sarah knew he would keep doing whatever he wanted, especially if he got a reaction.

She checked the labelling and the weight of each parcel, made sure that it was in the right delivery pile and with a cheerio to the ground crew, made her way back to the company van.

The long-term car park was adjacent to the company hangar, and as Sarah prepared to leave, she was surprised to see Joel wheeling his luggage through the parking bays to where he had left his vehicle.

"Hi there, stranger. I thought you'd deserted us. How was your trip?"

He looked around, clearly surprised. When he saw where the voice was coming from, he left the luggage alongside his vehicle and strolled over to where she was parked.

40

"Sarah! I wasn't expecting to run into you but given where we are, perhaps I should have." With one hand on his hip, he gestured with the other. "It was a productive trip, but exhausting. I'm keen to get back into the harness here and to apply my new knowledge."

"It must be a lot to take in. Couldn't you have discussed it all over the phone?"

To her discerning eyes, he did look tired. He raked his fingers through his hair distractedly. "It's useful attending to some things in person. It's not always easy from a distance and there were family matters to sort out."

"No trouble, I hope?"

"Nothing I can't deal with." There was a finality to his tone that didn't invite further comment.

He leaned with one hand against the van, capturing her within a bubble of intimacy. As she looked up at him, she was reminded again of just how tall he was—and how charismatic.

"Been dancing on any tables lately?" he inquired.

Sarah stifled a wince. Did he have to bring that up? "Been involved in any pub brawls lately?"

He laughed. "Touché. Fortunately, not. Anything otherwise of note happened around Alice while I've been away?"

"Nothing wildly exciting, except my friends Alex and Kathy are back from their honeymoon in New York, with heaps of stories. They've invited everyone out to Mulga Downs next weekend for a barbecue and a post wedding and honeymoon debrief."

"And where's Mulga Downs?"

"Head out of town, up the Stuart Highway and watch out for the turn off to the right about an hour up the road. Keep going for another couple of hours and you'll be there."

"That's a bit far to go for a barbecue, isn't it? You'd barely arrive when you'd have to turn around and come back again." Joel looked as incredulous as he sounded.

"Not too far around these parts—no. But we don't just go for the day. People take a swag or make other arrangements and make a night of it. There's some accommodation associated with the property, and others just unroll their swag and camp." Sarah looked at him speculatively. "It sounds as though you're going to be really busy, but if you're not tied up over the weekend, you could come too. It would give you the opportunity to see a working station. You'd understand your listening audience a little better."

"Well that's a point," he agreed "but I wouldn't be comfortable barging in on your friends like that. They don't know me from a bar of soap."

"They might not know you, but you know what the grapevine is like in Alice—by now they would know *of* you." Sarah wasn't going to disclose that she had done most of the telling. "It'll be a very informal affair and you've already met some of the people who'll be there. Chris and Mark for instance."

"The chopper pilots—I'd like to catch up with them again."

She twiddled one of her curls around her fingers, picking her way through her thoughts. "I tell you what—I'll give Kathy a call and explain to her you're doing background research on Centralian life as part of the induction to your new job, and that you'd like to get a better understanding of how stations operate. I'm driving out, so you can hitch a ride if you want. There'll be heaps of other people driving out if the timing doesn't suit. I'm leaving late morning on Saturday."

"It's tempting, but I've only just flown in. I'll have to check with the office first and see what commitments have arisen in my absence. Can I call you?"

"Sure." She pointed the key remote at the company van, clicking the unlock button. If she didn't look at him she could more easily feign indifference. "I must head back to town. The boss will think I'm lost. Let me know what you decide and I'll tell Kathy and Alex that you might be coming too. Give me a call through the week at the StationAir office."

Sarah scribbled the number on a piece of paper and handed it to him. Joel took it with a nod of acknowledgement. She watched him fold it and put it in his back pocket. It was time to make her exit.

"My chariot awaits. Catch you later."

She gave him a wave as she drove off with what she hoped was just the right degree of nonchalance. She suppressed her grin of triumph until she'd cleared the airport gates. It hadn't been too difficult after all. Great luck, running into him like that. Part of her wanted to call Kathy with an update but the other part didn't want to jinx her chances.

A couple of days later, her phone rang at work. Sarah's heart lurched as she heard Joel's mellifluous tones at the other end of the line. She could understand why he'd ended up in radio. He had a voice loaded with promise. In some circumstances it could be considered seductive.

"Hi Sarah—Joel here."

"Oh—you mean Joel, the radio manager cum interviewer extraordinaire?"

The immediate response was a snort. "The very one. Look if you're absolutely sure I won't be intruding, I'd like to come to Mulga Downs with you. I want to do some syndicated stories on outback life for the parent company that owns the radio station. It will be an opportunity to meet some locals and to perhaps tee up some interviews."

"It would be the right place for you to do that," she agreed. "You'll meet people who wouldn't normally be in town." She paused before continuing, her voice not so confident. "It would be company for me on the drive as well."

He laughed. "You read my mind. It's a win on all levels."

It was all Sarah could do not to giggle to herself on hearing that. She almost missed what he said next.

"The local colour and atmosphere will be great background for the recordings. I won't run around shoving microphones in people's faces but might get the odd recording here and there if that isn't intruding."

"Of course, not. It will be a good idea to watch and listen for a while though if you want to get people's trust, particularly as you're the new boy in town."

"Point taken, and I'm sensitive about that. Trust and confidentiality are important in my job. What time are you leaving and what should I bring?"
~

The drive out was uneventful. It was incredibly dusty once they left the bitumen, but as there was a clear road ahead of them, they left a dust trail instead of driving into one. There was one heart-stopping moment when a kangaroo bounded across the road, to be followed moments later by its mate, leaping from the roadside scrub. Sarah swerved to avoid it, losing traction momentarily on the loose surface.

"Sorry," she said after regaining control. "I should have eased off when I saw the first roo. When there's one, there's usually another not far behind."

"I'll keep that in mind," said Joel dryly. "I can add it to my list of local experiences."

Sarah flicked him a quick glance. What was already on the list? She had no intention of asking but her imagination ran riot. He stared straight ahead giving no quarter.

A little further on, an emu scarpered ahead of them, weaving from side to side before veering off into the bush. As

Sarah explained, they weren't such a problem on the roads. It was rare to hit them.

It was still early afternoon when they rumbled over the cattle grid at the front gate and drove up the long driveway leading to the homestead. It wasn't quite an avenue, but Alex's mother, Rose had planted a row of eucalypts along each side of the driveway, and indigenous shrubs filled in the lower storey. It created a welcoming entrance and a corridor for local birds and animals. The garden beyond was well tended, as best as could be maintained in a place that relied on bore water. The rain water tanks served the needs of the household.

As they unloaded their overnight bags from the rear of the vehicle, a screen door slammed. Sarah looked around to see Alex striding towards them.

"Sarah—good to see you could make it." He gave her a welcoming peck on the cheek and turned to Joel, hand outstretched.

"G'day. I'm Alex. You must be Joel. Kathy said you were coming. Welcome to Mulga."

"Yes. No hiding in these parts, is there? Thanks for letting me gate-crash your home-coming event. I hope you don't mind me taking a look around your place." The two men exchanged a firm handshake whilst looking each other over. *Just like dogs sniffing each other's bums. Glad they don't actually do that.*

Alex stiffened. "So long as you don't get in the way or interrogate my guests. There's plenty to look at here at Mulga."

"Not my style." With a fixed smile, Joel held up his hands in surrender mode.

Alex had never been known for his exuberance, though he was more relaxed once you got to know him. Sarah knew he would be stand-offish with Joel until he had the measure of the other man.

"Kathy's inside," he said in Sarah's direction. "She and Mum are driving the kitchen side of things. Make yourselves at home."

He strode off towards his ute, his faithful Red Heeler falling into place behind him. As Alex slid into the front seat, Rusty jumped into the back, bracing himself against the rough ride.

Sarah turned to the people already gathered to see who else had arrived and assembled on the front veranda. Chris and Mark were there already, and Brian from StationAir. She recognised some of the station hands and a couple of people from neighbouring properties. No doubt others would arrive shortly.

"Who invited you two pair of reprobates?" she inquired sweetly as she strolled over to where Chris and Mark were gasbagging with the others. She hadn't told them Joel was coming and the looks of quickly hidden surprise indicated her passenger was indeed unexpected. Mark glanced questioningly at Sarah, causing her to redden and look away. *I don't have to explain myself to anyone.*

"Well look who it is", he said. "The dancing sugar plum fairy."

Her glare should have killed at twenty paces, but it only caused him to laugh. Teasing Sarah had always been a bit of sport. He turned his attention to Joel. "Ma-a-a-te," he drawled, with an outback affectation. "You could have flown out with me in airborne comfort in a fraction of the time instead of driving out through the heat, the dust, and the flies in that poor excuse Sarah has for a car."

Joel grinned good-naturedly. "Another time I would love to, but my chauffeur has a few attractive attributes which you're obviously lacking. Anyway, the drive out was all part of the experience. Wouldn't have missed it for quids."

So what was the greater attraction; the novelty of the drive or my company? Sarah wasn't sure of the answer. "Who else is coming today?" she asked keen to know who might be around for a catch-up later.

"All the usual crowd I should think," responded Mark. "They'll probably straggle in for a while yet. Steve Jonas has just arrived from Plenty River. I don't expect to see Melissa Gilbert here though."

There were nods of agreement. Melissa had grown up on neighbouring Plenty River Station and had known Alex from childhood. She had always assumed their friendship would evolve into something more. The situation was sensitive, and Sarah quickly took control of the conversation. "She may not even be in the Territory at the moment. She seems to spend a lot of time in the big smoke. I think she has work interests there. I'm sure she'll have lots of time in which to catch up with the happy couple."

"Pity," muttered Chris quietly. "There's someone else she could have set her sights on."

"What are you muttering about, mate?" Mark asked.

"Nothing," said Chris. "Nothing at all."

"Usual state of affairs, then. Who's for a beer?"

More chiacking followed, all of it on a friendly level. Guests dumped their swags and some helped themselves to the first cold beer of the day. It was just the thing to wash away the dust of the road. It also allowed those who hadn't been there before, time to take stock of their surroundings.

The station had a building housing the staff quarters. These comprised individual rooms, with basically a bed, a chest of drawers and a desk. There was also a separate kitchen with attached dining/living area and ablution and laundry facilities. It was all very basic and the furniture had seen better days but it was still comfortable.

"Got your accommodation sorted?" Chris asked Joel and Sarah. "It's a case of first in, best dressed, especially if you want to be close to the bathroom facilities."

"You know," said Mark conspiratorially with a wink in Chris's direction, "some of us drink so much, they can't sleep through without having a nature call in the middle of the night. Not naming any names of course."

"Not my problem," responded Sarah. "I'll be sleeping in a guest room in the big house."

The sprawling wide-roofed bungalow had been added to over the years and Rose Woodleigh ensured her guest rooms were both well-appointed and comfortable. It was more luxurious than where the men would be sleeping. She banished the guilty thoughts. They would survive.

"Joel, I suggest we go and find Kathy, and I'll introduce you. We can get our accommodation sorted and then re-join everyone after that."

She turned back to the group. "We'll catch up after we've got ourselves settled. Don't drink all the beer."

Glasses were raised in good-natured salute, and the group turned back to their own discussions. Sarah and Joel headed around to the rear entrance of the homestead. As Alex had indicated, Kathy was busy in the kitchen, immersed in salads and food preparation, all under Rose's watchful eye.

"Okay if we come in?" she queried, pausing at the door.

"You're here," Kathy beamed. She gave Sarah an awkward hug, careful not to touch her friend's clothes with her messy hands. "And you must be Joel. I won't shake—my hands are covered in flour. I've heard a lot about you."

Sarah, whose hands were not so encumbered, managed to give Kathy an indignant dig in the ribs under the cover of the hug. Kathy's smile, focussed in Alex's direction did not react to the assault on her person.

Joel laughed. "It's probably all lies. I've heard a bit about you too, and so far it's all good." He turned to Rose, who was just taking a tray of scones out of the oven. "Mm—I thought something smelled good. I'm Joel."

"Pleased to meet you. I'm Rose Woodleigh. I thought people might be peckish after their drive. I know the men are probably kicking off with a beer, but I still find that my scones disappear reasonably quickly. Kathy dear, put the kettle on and I'll make a pot of tea."

"That reminds me," said Sarah. "I bought a few supplies out from Alice with me, including some of mum's apricot jam so that will go very well with your scones." She unloaded her shopping bag on the table. "We might dump our bags and get sorted Kathy, if you can point us in the right direction. After that, I'll come back and see if you need any help."

"You've timed your arrival rather well, because we're about done here. There's some cleaning up to do, but by the time you've found your rooms, we should be finished. Sarah, you're in the same room you occupied on your last visit. Joel can take one of the rooms out the back." She pointed Sarah and Joel in the direction of the staff quarters.

"Head out the back door and to the left. You'll see the accommodation block past the old stables. Can't miss it. Sarah, you take him down there. Pick out whichever room you want, Joel. Have a quick check around for any snakes but the doors have been closed except for when I flipped the mattresses and turned on the air-conditioning earlier."

Joel's eyebrows lifted slightly, but he refrained from comment.

"Thanks Kathy. It's good of you and Alex to let me gate crash your home-coming like this. I really appreciate the opportunity to see more of the local region."

"You're most welcome. We can always do with some sane and sensible input around the place to counter-balance the absurdity we otherwise encounter."

"I hope you're not referring to me with that last remark," said Sarah, her face a picture of mock indignation. "Come on Joel; we'd better leave Kathy to get on with it. I'll show you the quarters and you can take your pick of the rooms." She picked up her bag. "I'll see you in a while." She flung the last comment over her shoulder as she guided Joel out the door, but not before observing the juicy wink that Kathy threw in her direction.

Chapter 5

WHEN SARAH AND Joel emerged from their respective rooms, they found a handful of other visitors had adjourned to an assortment of seating on the front veranda. The lure of tea and hot scones had seen the cold beer set aside for later in the day, and the gossip centred on local characters, fuel prices, cattle prices and the export industry.

More car loads of visitors arrived. Sarah contemplated the scene in front of her. *Not much ever changes.* She was really looking forward to hearing some of the New York stories.

A small cloud of dust heralded Alex's return. He pulled up in his usual spot, and Rusty leapt off the vehicle and raced ahead of his master to greet the group and eye off whatever was edible. Gatherings on the veranda meant afternoon tea and therefore tasty titbits. The dog knew that. People were more than happy to share, caving in to the big, brown, pleading eyes, and then being rewarded with a grateful tail thump.

"Where've you been?" enquired Kathy as she exchanged a quick kiss for a cuppa and a plate with a couple of scones.

Alex lifted his hat slightly allowing cool air to flow across his scalp and wiped at the sweaty grimy rim that marked the hat's previous position. "Number Three Bore needed some adjustment. I'll be moving some cattle into that paddock through the week and had to be sure that water was available." He gulped his tea. "All I have to do now is collect some firewood for tonight. I don't suppose there are any volunteers for firewood duty?"

His expression as he surveyed the relaxed group in front of him was expectant.

"Just point us in the right direction, tell us what you need and we'll get it done," Chris said. "How much wood did you have in mind?"

"If we load up the tray on the back of the ute, that should keep us going. I've got gas for the barbecue but I thought we might build a bonfire as well. It's not fire ban season so we can have an open fire."

"Great thinking. Nothing like a good fire." Chris rounded up a few volunteers.

Joel joined the group too. "Count me in. I'll be happy to help."

"Well you men can go and get the wood, and I'll stay here with Kathy," said Sarah. "She can fill me in about the clothes and the shops and all the wonderful restaurants she patronised in New York. I want to hear it all."

"Lord, spare me" cried Mark. "I'll collect firewood as well."

There was general laughter and once the scones were gone, the men disappeared in a couple of vehicles. Kathy and Sarah cleared up the detritus from the afternoon tea, after which they disappeared to Kathy's bedroom to inspect the purchases.

"So," Kathy said conspiratorially, "what's your plan of action with Mister tall, dark and handsome? I can see the appeal. If I weren't a recently married woman, I might give you a run for your money."

"Don't give me that, Kathy. There's no way you would look at anyone else except Alex and for your information, I do *not* have any plan. Joel and I are just friends. I'm happy for it to stay that way."

"Is that so? Are you trying to fool me or fool yourself?"

Sarah drew herself up, trying to think of an effective response. The trouble was, she didn't really have one.

"Okay, don't bother answering. Look at what I bought instead. I still think you should have a plan though."

Sarah folded her arms, with a mock ferocious glare.

"Okay, okay, I won't say anything more."

By the time the men returned, Kathy had paraded her purchases, Sarah had admired them, and they had indulged in the sort of gossip that flowed more freely without the blokes being around.

"The shopping in New York is obviously great. I am seriously jealous."

"You should have seen Alex while I was cruising the stores. He was beside himself—not a cow in sight."

Kathy seemed very happy. Who would have thought that after all the tension-charged conflict that existed when she and Alex first met, they would form a partnership that was oh-so-right? They each had a steely determination which could have polarised them, but it appeared they were going to work well together instead. Sarah sighed inwardly. Once, she thought a relationship like that was to be her future as well. Sometimes, life sucked.

"We'd better see what's happening outside," Kathy said. "We'll need to set the tables up and gather a few chairs."

Some serious wood un-loading was happening when the two women ventured outside again. There were debates about how best to stack the pile, the burning times of different types of wood, and who should operate the chain saw to cut the larger pieces into fire-sized lengths.

Sarah laughed. "Doesn't take much to entertain you lot, does it? While you're all engaged in chest beating, can I get a volunteer or two to carry out the trestle tables? That's on the assumption you want access to the food tonight?"

"No worries." Joel stepped forward, wiping his grimy hands on the back of his jeans. "Should I wash my hands first or will they just get dirty again?"

She reviewed them critically. "They are grubby. I think Rose will throw a cloth on the tables, but just to be sure, you'd better wash up first. There's a sink in the utility room that's just inside the back door. It's used for this purpose. C'mon—I'll show you."

Joel followed Sarah towards the back door. "We've got enough wood to fuel a bonfire in Hades," he said. "They're a fairly enthusiastic bunch of blokes. Had an interesting chat with Chris while we were out there."

"Really? What about?"

"Well you, in a round-about sort of way. He indicated he was surprised to see me here and I explained about researching for the program, sourcing contacts and ideas for future interviews—that sort of thing. He seemed to think I might be using and abusing your generous nature in order to further my career. That's what I deduced; he wasn't terribly explicit."

Sarah frowned as she pointed Joel in the direction of the hand basin and he soaped his hands into a frothy lather.

"Oh, and there was something about 'you've had enough trauma in your life' and if anyone gave you further grief, he'd cheerfully break their neck. About as subtle as a sledge hammer. What did he mean?"

Her heart sank. She avoided Joel's gaze as she opened the back door. What did Chris think he was doing? She didn't need anyone to stand up for her, thank you very much. *I'm not ready to discuss my past with Joel. I don't need that complication.* She sensed an invading flush of mortification and took a deep breath and exhaled, willing the heat to dissipate before looking up at him.

"What a sweetie," she said brightly, deflecting from her real feelings. "Chris and Mark take a brotherly interest but I wish sometimes they would just butt out. I'm quite capable of taking care of myself—on the assumption there's any need of course, and I'm sure there isn't." She grabbed a towel from the rail behind the door. "Here's a towel. When you've finished, I'll be under the pergola where the barbecue is located. That's where we'll set up the trestles."

She made an escape before being quizzed any further on what Chris had said, or rather what he'd left unsaid. She didn't need him interfering in her life, no matter how well-intentioned. She only just caught Joel's muttered undertone, probably not meant for her ears.

"Brotherly interest, is it? Well there's a name for interests like that!"

Someone in the crowd declared it must be beer o'clock. Shadows grew longer and the intense heat of the day dissipated. Nobody had to drive anywhere that night, and the mood noticeably relaxed. Cartons of beer had been kept cold in the station cool room. On cue, Rose appeared with trays of nibbles to keep appetites at bay before the barbecue was ready. Kathy and Sarah opted for gin and tonics while Rose was happy with a sherry.

Earlier, Alex rigged up a screen under a shaded part of the gazebo. The area was just dark enough for he and Kathy to run through a display of some of the photos they had taken on their trip, giving a commentary as they went. They had seen all the usual highlights and a few more besides. They each had their favourite recollections, and agreed that American meals were huge. Alex was adamant the Mulga Downs steak was far superior. General comments from those present assured him there would never be any doubt on that score. The highlight for both was the helicopter trip over the Big Apple. Seeing the Statue of Liberty face to face was, as Kathy said, absolutely amazing.

"That trip even made me think about getting a helicopter licence," she said "and I never thought I would concede that to you two," she added in the direction of Chris and Mark.

"You'll never be in our league, Princess," crowed Mark, "but the flight must have been spectacular. I'm even a little bit jealous."

"There are interesting dynamics here," Joel murmured to Sarah. "I'm beginning to get a better understanding of the various personalities."

"It's not too difficult really. What you see is what you get. We're a fairly straightforward group."

Joel gave her an enigmatic look, but didn't comment any further.

"I reckon it's time to fire up the barbecue." Alex's pronouncement brought a bustle of activity.

"You get it going then," said Kathy, "and I'll start bringing out the food.

Those who weren't on barbecue duty set about the important task of setting and lighting the bonfire. It was well away from the house and any other structures which might be in danger from flying embers, but close enough to the facilities and the supply of drinks. Kerosene lamps had been hung from the trees, ready to be lit when it was properly dark.

Soon, sizzling was happening on the barbecue plate, and different opinions were offered on when to turn the meat for best effect. Sarah had long since learned never to get in the way of a man with a pair of barbecue tongs in his hand. The steaks and sausages were cooked perfectly, in spite of the self-professed experts, and heaped platters were soon available, along with fried onions and crispy potatoes.

There was something about the smell of a bush barbecue that was truly tantalising, or so Rusty and his mates seemed to think. The station kelpies, all working dogs, knew when not to encroach on the homestead but the pleading looks on their faces indicated that this was pure torment.

"Here, Rusty—come on boy." Sarah couldn't ignore those looks any longer. She noticed more than one visitor that night, who surreptitiously slipped a piece of sausage or steak in the dogs' direction. The lucky recipient devoured it in a single gulp while the others looked on enviously. The humans enjoyed the meal as well, as general chat and banter died down while people engaged in the serious business of eating.

Sarah ensured she introduced Joel to everyone, and tried to include him in the general conversation. It gave him the opportunity to talk about his job, and what he wanted to achieve with the interviews.

"Joel, you should have a chat to Tom Daly," said Alex. "He's the oldest one here by far and there's not much that's gone on over the years that Tom doesn't know about."

"Hey Tom," called Sarah. "You could be a radio star."

"Hmph," Tom sniffed. "Nobody's much interested in what I've got to say."

This comment caused general mirth because once he got going, Tom could talk the hind leg off a donkey. He'd chat to anyone who sat still long enough to listen and he loved an audience. The group had a lot of respect for the old man, as well as for his memory and knowledge of what went on in the region. He rarely ventured further than Alice Springs, so his understanding was limited by those Centralian boundaries.

"That New York must be pretty big," said Tom "but I don't reckon they've got steaks as good as this. Feast fit for a king this is."

Someone tried to point out that it should be 'fit for a queen' given that Elizabeth was the reigning monarch, but Tom didn't change his view.

"I know what I mean and I mean what I say," he growled. "This 'ere tucker 's as good as you'll get anywhere, if not better." No one was inclined to disagree.

With the meal taken care of and the remains cleared away or fed to the dogs, the crowd moved closer to the fire, taking chairs and milk crates to sit on. The flames had burned down, giving the pyromaniacs among them the chance to poke at it with long sticks, and to pile some choice logs on top. The lanterns were lit, and one of the stockmen brought out his guitar. His voice was melodious against the backdrop of the night, and others sang along when there were songs they knew. Tom joined in with his harmonica.

During those times when the music stopped, the sounds of the bush took over. There were night birds, the dogs occasionally huffed and snuffled, and crickets chirruped in the grass. At one stage there was an eerie howl.

"Bloody hell! What was that?" exclaimed Joel.

"Not quite the Hound of the Baskervilles," said Sarah. "Just a dingo, staking claim to his territory, or calling a mate or something like that. Their howl is quite spine-chilling. It's alarming when you don't know what it is."

"You're not wrong there." He leant back looking up at the sky. "There must surely be more stars here than back in town."

"I think you'll find there's the same number sitting over Alice, or Melbourne for that matter. You can just see them more clearly here. If you come away from the fire and the lights, you'll see even more. Come on—I'll show you."

Sarah jumped up and led Joel away from the fire and down towards the creek that wound close to the homestead. The noise around the bonfire faded and instead they began to hear the noises of the night and local landscape. They didn't have to go far before the darkness enveloped them. There was still the moon, a waning crescent shape, but their attention was taken by the belt of silver sparkles above them.

Sarah leaned back to better take in the heavens. As Joel stood behind her, it seemed only natural that she leaned into him. His arms slid around her, supporting her as he also tilted his head to examine the Milky Way. She was conscious of the warmth from his body. She had forgotten how good that could be and cherished the moment, not wanting it to stop.

"Did you know," she said, "the local aborigines had their own names for the stars. They have important significance in the Dreamtime stories, and falling stars are the means by which some of the wise men are able to bring stories to the people. They also know that as different stars appear or move to different positions in the sky, this heralds different seasons or events. Those old people were astronomers too."

"It seems to me you could give Tom a run for his money with some of the things you know." Joel was silent for a moment. "I know some stories about the stars as well."

"Do you? What sort of stories?"

"We-e-ll … if you kiss a girl under the stars, then it's the most amazing good luck for the future." Gently, he dropped a kiss on the top of her head. "Sarah, why don't you turn around so that I can kiss you properly?"

She froze, trying to gather her thoughts. Was she ready for this? After all the fantasising, the thought of kissing another man filled her with apprehension. It was almost a betrayal.

"Good luck for whom?" she whispered. "For you or for me?"

"I rather think it's good luck for both of us, don't you?" He dropped another kiss on her head and taking her firmly by the shoulders, turned her around. Tilting her chin up so that her face met his, he gently nibbled at the corners of her mouth—sensing, tasting and teasing. It felt good. It felt right.

She began to relax and melt towards him. It was only then that drawing her even closer, he claimed her mouth with passion and promise.

"You've no idea how much I've wanted to do that," he said, his voice husky. "I thought I was never going to get you alone. I've been thinking about it all evening."

At that proximity, the strength of his desire was hard to miss. "Perhaps you should have just asked," she said softly. "Sometimes the direct approach is the best."

"Perhaps, but I kinda think that how it happened has been rather nice, don't you?"

"You're probably right... so you had better kiss me again."

Sarah wrapped her hand around his neck, drawing his head closer. Her head swirled with emotion.

Delicious. This is just as delicious as I thought it might be. I so want this man. So why am I feeling so afraid?

"Tell me," he said as he lifted his lips from hers. "Your place or mine tonight?"

Chapter 6

WHEN THEY RETURNED to the camp fire, with Joel's arm slung around her shoulder, it didn't go unnoticed. She saw Chris and Mark exchange a wordless look. Neither man looked particularly happy. Mark gave a resigned shrug.

Kathy's response was a little more enthusiastic. She broke into a broad grin and gave Sarah a wink and thumbs up behind Joel's back. Alex was engrossed in conversation and didn't notice a thing. He wouldn't have cared anyway.

The beer gave way to rum for some, and port or liqueurs for others. Sarah, determined that Joel was going to see only the sober side of her this evening, was quite abstemious, nursing her drink carefully. She leaned into him relishing the support of his arm around her. The contact was a commitment and a promise.

He nuzzled into her hair. "Do you know how good you smell? Sort of smoky and night-fresh and countrified."

"Is that really a smell? Perhaps I could market it if it's tantalising to a man. The scintillating scent of country woman."

"Mm—it sure does it to me. It's like a promise of good things to come."

Sarah was glad that the low light hid the glow which tingled all over. How soon could they decently make their excuses and depart for their own private party? Would anybody miss them if they quietly slipped off? Most were too engrossed in their yarns. Still, the anticipation in itself was delightful.

The stories danced over and around the fire, as tales were recounted of local exploits and of course fantastical travels. New York featured, but everyone seemed to have their own travel tale and regaled the group at large with the telling, probably better than the reality.

It had been a long day for some, and progressively the crowd thinned as people crept away into swags, or else to their rooms in the staff quarters. Conversation petered, and those who were left lapsed into companionable silence, occasionally broken by a persistent story teller. Alex gave the fire one last poke, sending sparks skywards before handing the stick to Joel.

"Well mate, I think you're in charge of the fire now. It's about time I hit the sack. Plenty to do tomorrow. I'll see you in the morning." He turned to Kathy. "See you when you come in, sweetheart."

"I'm right behind you," Kathy said, stifling a yawn. "I've enjoyed catching up with everyone, but now it's catching up with me. I'm for bed too."

With another wink in Sarah's direction, she hoisted herself to her feet, stretched her cramped limbs, and ambled after her husband. The silences around the fire were getting longer, even with the diehards. A couple were well-known as stayers, and there was no way they were leaving until the rum was gone or the fire had burnt out through lack of wood. Given the size of the pile that remained, their heat source was not a problem. With an arm casually draped behind Sarah, Joel massaged the back of her neck.

"And what about you? You must be feeling tired after your long drive today."

"Mm—don't stop. That feels wonderful. I didn't realise how tight those muscles were until you touched them."

"The man with the miracle fingers—that's me. You'd be amazed at what they can do." He whispered quietly, for her ears alone.

"Would I now? I might have to put that to the test. I think there are parts of me that could really use a miracle."

"The pleasure would be all mine." He poked at the fire, sending sparks flying and causing pockets of flame to flare up. "Are you feeling sleepy? Perhaps it's time you retired as well."

"Perhaps you're right. C'mon." Sarah rose and beckoned Joel to follow her, with the fire stick being passed on to one of the stayers. Their departure did not raise much interest at all.
~

"Shh. Tread quietly." Taking his hand, Sarah led Joel down the central passage of the homestead towards her allocated room. A floor board creaked and she froze, stifling the urge to giggle. She sidestepped closer to the outer edge of the passage, hoping the boards there would be quieter.

"Is that you, Sarah?" Rose's muffled voice came from behind a closed door.

"Yes, only me. See you in the morning."

Sarah hoped she sounded nonchalant. She wasn't. Far from it.

Softly, hardly even daring to breathe, they continued creeping down the passage. She should have known Rose would hear, and Sarah blushed slightly as she thought of what she was doing. Joel would have to be up and into his own quarters very early.

At the door to her room, she fumbled for the light switch and pulled Joel in behind her, shutting the door quietly. He reached for her and embraced her tightly, devouring her in hot, hungry kisses. They stumbled towards the bed, and half collapsed, half eased onto it as the effort to remain upright became too much.

Sarah could feel her level of passion rising, and with her hands grasping his butt cheeks, pulled him close to her, anxious to feel all of him. *I never thought I'd feel this way again. It's been so long. Dave, my love, don't hold this against me.*

With a small moan, Joel slid a hand up under her shirt, gently kneading the soft mound within his grasp.

She closed her eyes, relishing the butterflies that were dancing a fandango from her breasts and moving in a downward spiral. To be so close to a warm body evoked so many memories. She was drowning in a molten pool of heady physical and emotional response. Joel wasn't the only one to be aroused by the smell of another body in close contact. She inhaled deeply relishing that man smell and what it did to her.

It wasn't according to script when Joel broke off contact mid-kiss. Her eyes jolted open. Grasping her shoulders, Joel pushed her back so he could look at her face, his expression a mixture of earnest and sad.

"Sarah, you're doing the most incredible things to me, but I can't do this."

The loss of contact left her shocked and bewildered. She gaped at him, bereft and unable to understand what had just happened. "What do you mean? Can't do what?"

"I can't creep into someone's house like a thief in the dark. It's seedy. And there's no way that I'm taking you back to my single room with those squeaky bed springs. The sound would carry for miles. When I make love to you, I want it to be drawn out and special—luxurious even. Not some illicit snatched moment like a couple of teenagers in a place I've no right to be."

Sarah stared at him wordlessly. He was right of course. It was wrong of her to bring him into her room. It was an abuse of Rose's hospitality. Knowing what was right and abiding by it were two different things. A feeling of abandonment overwhelmed her as Joel eased himself quietly from the bed, kissed her briefly and picked up his shoes.

"I'll see myself out. You stay here. Sleep tight and hold those thoughts. We'll find the right time and place of our choosing, I promise."

The door shut softly behind him, leaving Sarah with mixed emotions. The pulse in the core of her being was a heightened sensation she hadn't thought she would feel again. It was dangerous because of where it could lead. Commitment was not on the agenda. Commitment left you vulnerable. If you were vulnerable, the very worst could happen. She understood that so well.

There was no denying the throbbing ache though. Right now, her body was screaming. Screaming for the touch and warmth and relief it craved. She sat up, her lips feeling bruised from the recent encounter. She could feel her heart thumping as she strained to hear the muffled sounds of Joel's departure—out of her bed, out of the house, and out into the night.

What would Dave think if he could see her now? Was he watching? *I'm not ready. Not yet. It's just over a year.* To make love with Joel at this stage of their relationship was moving too fast—faster than her comfort level—and she was so scared of jinxing things.

She had been caught up with the romance of the stars and the proximity of his body and that man scent. How long had it been since a man had tantalised her senses like that? Too long or not long enough?

She eased herself off the bed and peeled her clothes off, leaving them where they fell. She cupped her breasts with her hands, feeling their rounded fullness. "Beautiful," Dave used to say. "You have the most beautiful breasts."

The cool night air tingled her skin as she slid her hands down over her belly, remembering the sensation of his hands caressing her—teasing, tantalising, tormenting—memories she had repressed. Her hands slid lower making a soft downy contact. A strangled sob escaped her. It was so unfair. "Why did you leave me?" she whispered into the darkness.

But who did she mean?

Angrily, she pulled out her nightclothes from the overnight bag and tugged them on. She wanted to cover herself and the body holding so many painful memories.

When she padded down to the bathroom moments later, the house was quiet, disturbed only by a lone Mopoke that called from outside. Its lonely haunting cry reflected her distress.

The smell of bacon lured Sarah from her bed in the morning. Still in her PJs, she padded up the hallway and into the kitchen. Rose's domain was the hub of the house. It was large, accommodating not only masses of storage cupboards but a scrubbed wooden table that could fit a host of people. There was another dining room, but this was the place of informal eating and where the day started.

A pantry lead off to one side, and a cool room was adjacent to the back veranda. During action time at the station, the kitchen became an operations centre, keeping hearty appetites fed and sustained. Large windows looked out over the kitchen garden, providing natural light. Those working over a hot stove or the kitchen sink didn't have to feel shut off from the world.

Rose orchestrated wonderful things as eggs, bacon and toast emerged in coordinated fashion around her, seemingly with no major effort. Two huge frying pans sat on the stovetop, one with sizzling rashers of smoky bacon. The other contained beaten eggs and milk, with a little butter and salt and pepper. She flipped the bacon with one hand while stirring the eggs with the other. The scene depicted years of experience. Kathy laid out plates and accoutrements of what looked to be a wonderful meal.

"Morning Sarah," called Rose, glancing over her shoulder and then returning to her stirring. "Did you sleep well? Tea's in the pot if you'd like to grab a cup."

"Slept like a log," she lied. "I thought I was still dreaming when that wonderful smell came sneaking into my bedroom. A cuppa would be wonderful," she added. "My throat is so dry. I must have inhaled a bonfire-worth of smoke last night."

Kathy handed her a mug with a smirk. "Did I hear two pairs of footsteps last night?" she queried softly. Louder, she said, "You might want to grab a shower soon while there's still some hot water."

Sarah glared at Kathy, indicating Rose's back with a nod. Irritatingly, Kathy just grinned.

All Sarah could do was roll her eyes. "I'll head for the bathroom shortly and then be back for some breakfast. If it tastes as good as it smells, it's going to be yummo."

Rose smiled. "There's plenty here when you're ready dear.

Sarah poured the steaming tea into the mug Kathy had given her from a catering-sized tea pot. No jiggling tea bags for Rose. Cupping the mug in her hands as she drank, Sarah drew comfort from its warmth. The morning wasn't cold, but still held an early freshness.

She wandered out the back door to size up the day. The clear sky promised plenty of sunshine, once the sun established itself.

The magpies in the adjoining trees seemed to think the day would be good, as they carolled and warbled to each other. One of them swooped down to the rear of the house and stole a cat biscuit from the bowl by the back door, before retreating to the safety of the tree. It wasn't at any risk from the cat, not with the size of that beak.

Sarah wondered how Joel had slept. All was quiet down towards the accommodation block so she had no idea whether or not he was awake. She contemplated knocking on his door, but decided against it. Let him sleep if that was what he was doing.

She drained the last of her tea and slipped back inside, before being sprung in her pyjamas.

~

Returning to the kitchen after her shower, Sarah found a cluster of people around the table. They looked remarkably spritely given the late night some for some of them. Judging by the dishes in the sink, some visitors had been and gone, though there were probably more to come.

"Sit yourself down, Sarah," said Rose. "This will keep you going for today."

She placed a plate of scrambled eggs and bacon in front of her and dropped a couple of slices of bread in the toaster. This was not pre-formed, pre-sliced supermarket bread. It was cut from a huge high-rise loaf that Rose had made. It was the sort of bread that had you coming back for more, even though you kidded yourself that you were on a diet and never ate it.

"Keep your eye on the toast and grab it when it's ready. Butter and jams are on the table. Sing out if you want anything else."

Joel sat at the table. He tackled his breakfast with gusto, his mouth full as he looked up. He nodded acknowledgement of her presence, not yet able to speak. Sarah slid into the chair opposite him, uncertain of her feelings. His eyes met hers over his coffee mug.

"Morning Sarah. I hope you slept well." When he finally spoke, his voice was tinged with a hint of tease.

"Yes of course. Thank you" She sounded prim. What else was she supposed to say anyway? *No, not really. I tossed and turned and thought about what did and didn't happen, and what never will again, and whether or not I really want it to happen anyway?* She didn't want to talk about it.

"Rose is coming into the studio to do an interview, next time she's in town," Joel said. "I came out here thinking about station operations and all that goes on in the cattle industry but watching Rose has made me realise there's another side to station life, and the women are the key to that." He sounded animated. "It should be a popular segment with the listeners, starting with when she first came to Mulga Downs as a new bride."

"I'm not sure people will be so interested," demurred Rose. "It's not anything special. It's a story repeated on any station around here."

"But Radio Alice is part of a larger network. I'm sure the locals *will* be interested in a day in the life of Rose Woodleigh, and to the listeners in the big cities, the story will be fascinating."

"What will be?" The slam of the screen door heralded Mark's arrival. His trademark sunnies were already perched on top of his head. "Morning Sugar Plum," he added, ruffling Sarah's curls as he passed—quickly enough to avoid her swipe in response.

"G'day Mark," said Joel. "I was explaining to Sarah that I'm arranging an interview with Rose to introduce the topic of women in the bush. Having seen her in action here has made me aware it's an aspect of station life I hadn't considered."

"Like I said," continued Rose. "It's nothing special. You just see what has to be done, and get on with it. Roll up your sleeves and you'll be fine."

"That's exactly what people will want to hear about."

"Well make sure you tell people what a great cook Rose is," Mark said. "Her apple pies are to die for. It's worth dropping in for lunch when we're working in this area. Chris and I often do."

"I haven't got past the scrambled eggs yet." Joel looked sadly at his plate, which was now empty except for some creamy crumbs. He had to make do with cleaning those up with a crust of toast.

Nothing wrong with one of his appetites, mused Sarah. *Maybe he didn't really fancy me?*

Mark fetched himself a heart-challenging plate of eggs and bacon, smothering his toast liberally with butter. No fears about the waistline for this man.

"Of course, the real action takes place in the air," Mark said, pausing between mouthfuls. "We see everything that's going on and have the flexibility to put down anywhere. I've found cattle that have been hiding up the back of beyond for years. There's been a fortune on the hoof that no-one knew about." He wiped a dribble of grease from his chin. "If you want to come up for a quick spin after breakfast, I'll show you."

"Really? That would be fantastic. I'll take the camera and get some good shots from the air as well."

"No probs. We can't go too far or I won't have enough fuel for the rest of the day but I can give you an idea of what it's all about. It's a clear morning so you should get some good photos. The rest is up to the photographer."

"I'll take full responsibility for that side of things. What time are you thinking?"

"About half an hour? Perhaps Sarah can run us down to the strip. The air is relatively calm at this time of day, so the flight won't be too bumpy."

"Great. I'll see you back here in thirty. I'll take a wander with my camera in the meantime. Is that okay with you, Sarah? Can you run us down to the airstrip?"

"Sure. I'll have finished my breakfast and cleaned up by then." *I don't mind running you around while you have your fun experiences. Why should I?*

"You're a sweetheart. Thanks for that." With a wink thrown in Sarah's direction, Joel rose and headed back to his room, the slap of the screen door signifying his departure. Mark made quick work of his breakfast also and disappeared to attend to his pre-flight paperwork.

No other breakfast customers were around, so Rose took advantage of that. "Call me if you need me, girls. I've got things to do—a load of washing for instance."

Kathy had been stacking dishes at the sink, but with everyone else gone she stopped and slid in next to Sarah who was still sitting in front of a half-eaten meal.

"So, Sarah—what's happening?"

"Well, it seems that I'm taking Mark and Joel out to the airstrip shortly."

"I know that. I heard. You know that's not what I mean. What's happening with you and Joel?"

"I don't know really."

"How can you not know?"

"We're just taking things slowly, okay? There's nothing to tell."

Sarah was more abrupt than she meant to be, but she wasn't ready for the cross-examination either. Even if she wanted to, there was nothing to report and she avoided looking at Kathy. She was confused herself. Perhaps she was she nothing more to Joel than an intro to the local community. Was she just a convenience?

"I'm sorry. Tell me where to get off. It's none of my business I know, but when things are going so well in your own life, you want to spread some of the happy juice around. I'd love there to be someone special for you too."

"Yeah, well... when there's something to tell, you'll be the first to know." Sarah put her dishes on the sink and fled back to her room. Normally she would have helped with the washing up, but not today. She understood Kathy's well-meaning interest but right now she was confused and hating herself for it. Joel's attention this morning had been only cursory. Did what happened between them last night mean nothing? Had he left her room because he'd changed his mind about her and not because he was concerned about Rose?

Her thoughts tangled in circles, with no outcome other than a mild stress-induced headache. Her last relationship ended in grief and this one wasn't even going to get off the ground.

There wasn't time to dwell on it as she needed to run the two men down to the airstrip. She cleared a few things off the rear seat of her vehicle to make way for another passenger and chatted to Rusty, who welcomed the attention.

Alex said Rusty was an excellent judge of character. The dog and Sarah already had a mutual admiration thing going, clearly demonstrated by some intense tail action and intermittent nudging, indicating that she could keep scratching behind his ears, thank you very much.

"Hope we haven't kept you waiting?"

Mark, closely followed by Joel, rounded a corner of the house and headed in her direction. *This will be interesting. How will Rusty react towards Joel?*

The dog, observing humans approaching, abruptly abandoned Sarah and launched himself at Mark in enthusiastic greeting. Mark was a frequent visitor to the property and so man and dog were well-acquainted.

"Got yourself a friend, mate?" Joel enquired, observing the canine enthusiasm. He stood, hands on hips. His camera was slung around his neck and he looked ready for action.

Pity he wasn't so ready last night. Sarah kept those thoughts to herself, castigating herself as she did for being unreasonable as she watched Mark's show of affection.

"Rusty and I go back a long way, don't we boy?"

A shrill whistle pierced the air. "Rusty!" bellowed Alex, opening the door of the station ute. "In the back."

The dog responded immediately, taking a flying leap into the tray of the vehicle. His whole demeanour indicated this was work time. With a cursory wave in their direction, Alex drove off. Station life waited for no one.

Joel slid into the front seat of the wagon beside Sarah and Mark took the rear. She drove the short distance to the strip, with Mark maintaining a monologue about the benefits of helicopters in country like this and of course his Robinson in particular.

The strip was unsealed but graded, with a surface of compacted gravel to help maintain serviceability in wet weather. Adjacent to the windsock was the platform holding a hand pump and couple of drums of Avgas, used for refuelling.

Chris was already there, readying his machine for take-off. Both pilots were flying a Robinson 22, small two-passenger machines which were popular for aerial mustering. Their speed and efficiency made up for the expense over a team of men on horseback or motor bike.

Chris had a job at a neighbouring station, and was heading off to make a start. Joel watched as Chris busied himself with refuelling his aircraft and Mark completed the daily inspection on his. He and Sarah stood well clear so as not to get in the way.

"These machines aren't very big close up, are they? I'm kind of reminded of an aerial mosquito." Joel remarked. "Slightly larger than a toy."

"Big enough for what they need to do," Sarah replied. They're different to the media-owned helicopters you're probably used to. The bigger they are, the higher the operating cost. A light manoeuvrable machine serves this purpose better."

"I can see that." He paused. "You're quiet this morning, sweetheart. Is everything okay?"

"Yes, of course. Bit tired perhaps. This is my Sunday morning persona, that's all."

He reached out and stroked her cheek. "I look forward to getting to know the personas for every day of the week. Sarah, I—"

"All aboard mate, cos I'm ready to go." Mark, hands on hips, was standing by the open door.

"Absolutely." He dropped a quick kiss on Sarah's cheek. "See you soon."

Under Mark's direction, Joel climbed aboard, strapped himself in and put on a headset. The noise at operating level ruled out normal conversation. The rotors began turning with a high-pitched whine. Sarah retreated a respectful distance from the dust she knew would be stirred up on take-off, and was joined by Chris.

"You two look to be getting cosy, Sugar Plum."

She turned to reprimand him, but left it. He'd call her whatever he wanted anyway. He always did. "Just good friends, Chris. Nothing to write home about."

"He seems a nice enough bloke, but be careful. He's new to town and you don't know that much about him."

"I don't think he's any great danger." She smiled. "He's probably more interested in his job than in me."

"Well, that's not altogether surprising."

"What do you mean by that?" *Was Chris suggesting she wasn't attractive? Did a job rate more highly than she did?* Puzzlement crept into her voice. "Why wouldn't he be interested in me?"

"No, no, no—that came out wrong. I didn't mean—of course any bloke would be interested in you, Sugar. You know what these media types are like though."

"Not really, no I don't. What are they like?" She was truly baffled.

Chris looked uncomfortable and avoided her gaze. "Well, you can't be sure which team he bats for can you?"

Sarah let out a deep belly laugh. The tension drained from her. Of all the things Chris could have said, this was least expected. "Chris, that's just so preposterous. Of course he's into women. I would know by now if it were any different."

"Yeah, okay, okay. It was just a thought. I care about you Sugar. You've had a rough trot in recent times and I wouldn't like to see you get hurt or led up the garden path."

"Chris, you're such a sweetie, and I understand where you're coming from but I'm a big girl. I know sometimes it can seem I've got my head in the clouds, but I don't take any steps lightly, particularly when it means getting involved with someone. I appreciate your concern though—really." *I just wish he'd shown some more interest in my garden.*

Impulsively, she gave Chris a hug. Even though what he had suggested was ludicrous, and the inference she needed some masculine protection irked her, she appreciated the care he expressed. She dropped a light kiss on his cheek, which to her surprise felt dry and hot.

"Hey, are you all right? You feel as though you're burning up."

"It's the effect you have on me Sugar—you set me on fire."

"You guys are so silly. I do so love you both."

"Why thank you ma'am—I think. Anyway now that Mark is off and away, I'd better get moving too. They'll think I've forgotten them at Plenty River."

"I doubt it. They know there was a gathering here so they probably don't even expect you yet." She looked critically at him, noting his overall pallor but rosy cheeks. "You even look flushed. Are you sure you're okay or are you embarrassed about something?"

"Me? Never. Just over-excited, that's all. I'll catch you later. Look after yourself." He clambered aboard his little machine and was soon airborne, doing a quick circuit of farewell and then climbing out on track for Plenty River.

Sarah waved him off and returned to the car. She wasn't sure how long Joel and Mark would be but didn't want to wait at the strip with only a few crows for company. They didn't talk much. Mark would buzz the homestead on their return flight, and she could come back to the strip then.

As she drove, Sarah reflected on what Chris had just suggested. Of course, it was ludicrous. Joel had kissed her, hadn't he? There was passion in that and he gave clear indication of being aroused. Still, now it had been stirred up, that little niggle of doubt persisted. Was that the reason Joel had pulled away and left her room last night? Did it have nothing to do with his sense of propriety?

Damn you Chris - why did you put such an idea into my head? She realised how little she knew about Joel beyond the here and now. She knew nothing of his previous life or past relationships or anything like that. She would have to ask him when the time was right, assuming she actually wanted to know.

Rose was already mixing up a batch of rock buns for morning tea and Kathy was finishing off the last of the dishes when Sarah returned.

"I won't get in your way Rose—I'm sure you have a much lighter hand with mixing batter than I have." She surveyed the collection of bowls and ingredients lined up on the kitchen bench. "Next time I come I'll remember to bring some of my grandma's strawberry jam. There would be a big demand for it here. Got a spare tea towel? I'll help with those dishes."

"Thought you'd never ask," quipped Kathy, throwing a tea towel in Sarah's direction. "When I said 'I do' I never imagined that it meant I'd be up to my elbows in soap suds on a Sunday morning."

Rose smiled to herself. Sarah was entirely unsympathetic.

"That's what you get if you marry a country boy," she teased. "Watch out; he'll have you out branding cattle next."

"No way. The cattle are his domain. I'll stick to my flying, thank you. My leave will be up all too soon, and then it's back into harness for me. I'm learning about cattle markets and prices and things like that, but not so sure about getting close up and personal with them. Those beasts are huge." Kathy paused before changing tack. "Everything okay down at the strip?"

"Yes. Chris was getting ready for his flight to Plenty, and Mark and Joel took off for their sight-seeing tour. They won't be too long They'll buzz the homestead on their return. Other than that, the strip was deserted." She put away a pile of clean dishes, looking back over her shoulder as she did. "There are a couple of other aircraft parked there but who in their right mind would leave before Rose's baking was out of the oven? That in itself will have the guys returning soon. Have you been refining your scone-baking techniques, Kathy?"

The response was a tea-towel flicked at her. The banter continued as the last of the dishes were put away, leaving only a clean-up of the kitchen area to be finished. It coincided with the rhythmic whump-whump-whump-whump over the roof, signifying the return of the chopper.

Sarah abandoned the tea towel and slipped outside waving acknowledgement to the faces peering out of the bubble as she made her way back to the car. As she set off for the strip, Mark and the chopper headed in the same direction.

"You were a bit low weren't you?" she called as the two men unbuckled and extricated themselves from the machine. Joel still had his camera slung around his neck. "I thought you were going to skewer yourselves on the radio mast."

"Not likely, sweetheart. You should know I'm more careful than that."

"A cowboy, more like it. So, Joel—how was your first chopper flight?"

Joel's grin as he approached Sarah said it all. "I got some fabulous shots. What a way to travel. It's got me hooked. I'll have to become a filthy rich media mogul now, just so I can afford my own chopper and pilot."

"Well you can start now with an ace chopper pilot," grinned Mark. "I have to warn you though—I don't come cheap."

"I'll keep that in mind. I'll focus on the research at Mulga Downs first and worry about being a mogul tomorrow. Who knows—my brilliant interviews and photography might attract the right attention." He turned back to Sarah, clipping the lens cap on his camera. "That was thirsty work. Do you think there'll be a cup of tea back in the kitchen?"

"There'll be more than that, judging by what I last saw. Should be ready by the time we get back."

Mark unrolled the fuel hose and dragged it closer to the chopper. "Is it okay if I just refuel first? I won't hold you up too much, will I? I'll need to head off shortly. Sarah, can you drop me back here again after I've grabbed my gear?"

"Of course. Do what you have to do." Sarah propped herself up against the side of her car and sent a hesitant smile in Joel's direction. "So—it's been a productive weekend then?"

"It's been a great weekend, on so many different levels. It will take me a while to feel really at home in Alice, but getting to know people this way makes a difference. I'm getting a better understanding of the place and what makes it tick."

He hasn't said that he's getting a better understanding of me. We still hardly know each other.

She spoke with an enthusiasm she didn't feel. "That's great. I'm glad I invited you. It seems to have paid off in relation to the contacts you've made."

"Yeah, but Sarah, it's not only about work. I've really enjoyed your company, but you know that don't you?" He reached out and drew her close dropping a light kiss on her forehead. "I wasn't expecting to meet you when I came to Alice."

"So, I'm just a bonus, am I?"

"You're a beautiful bonus and not *just* a bonus. I don't know where we're heading but I'm going to enjoy finding out. Don't you agree?"

She pulled back from his embrace so she could look him in the face. If he was sincere, she wanted to be able to see it for herself.

His smile reached the crinkle at the side of his eyes, but it only partly reassured her. Mark's approach saved her from answering.

"Thanks for waiting. It'll save me time when I need to go. We can get back to that cup of coffee now," Mark said.

Although it wasn't long since breakfast, the overnighters had clustered again on the front veranda. Alex and Rusty had returned as well. The group sprawled in the assortment of chairs, re-sharing some of the tales from the night before. Tom Daly had driven home early, but some of his reminiscences still earned a chuckle.

Everyone grabbed their brew of choice from the kitchen and ambled around to the front of the house. Rose had brought out a basket of freshly baked biscuits wrapped in a large cloth to keep them warm. People were free to help themselves. There was general discussion about making tracks and heading back to town or their home turf, but there was no hurry.

"It's yummy, Rose." Sarah licked her fingers appreciatively and rubbed at the streak of jam decorating her cheek. "I would eat another except I can't."

There was not much comment in response. Everyone else was too engrossed in eating. The phone could be heard ringing from inside the house, and Alex jumped up to answer it. Minutes later, the door to the house slammed and Alex re-appeared looking agitated. He removed his hat and wiped at the sweaty mark on his forehead where it had been sitting. He caught Mark's eye.

"That was Melissa Gilbert from Plenty River. She said Chris has been taken ill—very ill. He can't fly and he's been loaded into a vehicle and she's driving him back here so we can get him to town." He looked at his watch. "They should be here in about forty minutes."

Chapter 7

IT WAS A fast trip back to town—as fast as Sarah could safely manage on the unsealed portion of the road. There had been some debate about how to get Chris to the nearest medical facility back in Alice Springs. Mark offered to fly him, but Chris wouldn't hear of it.

"Mate, don't be stupid," he'd muttered, his face red and beaded with perspiration. "It's just some passing bug; not worth jeopardising our contract over."

He paused. The effort of speaking seemed to exhaust him. "You get on with the job and I'll be okay. I'll be right as rain tomorrow—be back before you know it. Gotta finish that job at Plenty."

"Don't worry about that," Melissa said. "I'll explain the situation to Dad. We'll sort something out. For now just get yourself better."

It's not like Melissa to be so compassionate, Sarah mused. *Quite out of character.*

She and Joel threw their overnight bags in the car, and after making quick farewells, hit the road. Joel took the back seat, giving Chris the greater comfort and leg-stretch in the front. Chris appeared to doze for most of the trip, only opening his eyes wide when Sarah hit a large pothole at speed, with the threat of becoming airborne.

"Sugar, at this rate you're going to kill me before anything else has a chance," he protested weakly.

"Don't you even think about dying," she retorted, "especially in my car. In this heat, it could become distinctly unpleasant."

"You're so caring. You've no idea what that means to me." He lapsed into his doze again.

At least he's still coherent. I've never seen anyone get so sick so quickly. She glanced at Joel in the rear-vision mirror. His sunglasses obscured any meaningful expression.

"Hope you're not too uncomfortable back there. I've probably hit some of the corrugations too fast. We should be back on the bitumen soon, and then it will be a smoother ride back into Alice."

"Don't worry—I've got my seatbelt done up hard and tight. As long as we get back in one piece, I'll be fine. Chris is our priority."

There speaks a sensible man. Is that what I need, a counterfoil to my impulsiveness? Or is that too yin for my yang?

By the time they approached the outskirts of Alice Springs, Chris muttered incoherently. Sarah had stopped a couple of times during the journey to wet a face washer with water from her water bottle, and wiped the perspiration from his face in an effort to cool him down. She angled the air vents to give him maximum exposure to the air conditioning, but he was still hot to the touch.

"I think I'll go straight to the hospital," she said to Joel. "I had intended to take him to the Medical Centre but his condition has worsened during the drive. This is beyond treatment from the local GP."

"Good idea. It looks to be more than 'just some bug'. Do you get malaria up this way?"

"There are plenty of mosquitos, but I've never heard of anyone getting anything nasty from them. Always a first time, I guess."

She pulled up at the front of the emergency department and Joel went inside in search of a wheel chair. With some effort, they manoeuvred Chris onto the seat. It was clear he wasn't capable of walking in and standing around until the triage staff were able to review him. His breathing was laboured, and he slumped down in the chair looking exactly what he was—a very sick man.

Sarah left Joel to wheel him inside, while she moved the car to the authorised car park. By the time she re-joined them, the two men had progressed to the front of the line at the triage counter. Joel was doing his best to answer the questions being thrown at him.

He looked at her with relief. "Here she is. Sarah will know that sort of detail. I don't even know his full name."

"Harris—Christopher Harris."

Sarah provided the information she had, which was sufficient for preliminary purposes. As directed, they wheeled Chris into an examination cubical, and managed to get him out of the chair and onto an examination bed. A nurse bustled in and recorded his blood pressure, pulse and temperature on a chart, before leaving, saying as she did a doctor would be with them shortly.

"I hope they don't keep us waiting too long," Sarah muttered. Not having anything else to hand, she wet some paper towel at the hand basin and mopped Chris's face again. "I'm trying not to be alarmist but I've never even known Chris to be sick before. It can't be food poisoning because he's not vomiting and the rest of us are fine."

"That's true. My only complaint is over-eating."

Sarah's threw him a quick frown in response. This wasn't the time for levity. "As far as I know, he's not been anywhere where he might come into contact with any contagious diseases. He spends a lot of time out bush. If he has a big mustering job, he stays on the station or in some instances, even camps out."

"I feel useless here," said Joel. "Why don't I get us a coffee while you channel Florence Nightingale? It's a long time since morning tea, and we didn't have time for lunch."

Now that he mentioned it, Sarah realised she was both hungry and thirsty. Getting Chris to town had been her primary focus. The inner woman had been ignored.

"Joel, that would be great. It will be canteen food but if there is anything edible I'll take it. Just something to take the edge off."

"I'll see what I can find. Back soon." He squeezed her shoulder briefly as he left. That touch made Sarah aware of the tightness she was carrying in those muscles. What she wouldn't give for a back massage. She hadn't noticed at the time, but she must have developed of stress-induced tension on the drive back to town. The speed at which she hit some of those potholes wouldn't have helped.

As she kneaded the back of her neck, the cubical curtain was pushed back and the doctor hurried in. She was a very short woman, looking tired and harassed, and who introduced herself as Doctor Kumar.

She reviewed the detail on the patient notes. "Mr Harris, can you tell me how you feel?"

Chris's eyes were open but were glazed and he did not respond. She addressed her queries to Sarah.

"When did the fever start? Has he been overseas recently? What work does he do? Where has he spent the last two weeks? Has he complained of a rash?"

While firing off these questions, she pulled up Chris's shirt and applied her stethoscope, tapping several times on his chest as she did so. She also checked under his eyelids and took a quick glance at the surface of his limbs. Sarah answered according to the knowledge she had.

"Is he on any medication?" Dr Kumar continued. "Does he use any recreational drugs?"

"No! Nothing like that. As far as I know, the fever only started this morning but his condition worsened rapidly," Sarah explained. "He's a helicopter pilot and does a lot of contract work—mustering and the like. That's all around the Centralian region though; he hasn't been overseas in a long time. No rash as far as I know."

"I'll admit him while we undertake further tests. I'll send some blood off to pathology and give him some IV fluids. Has he come into contact with many people?"

The curtain to the cubical was pulled aside and Joel returned, clutching two take-away coffees and a couple of Anzac Biscuits. He nodded to the doctor and handed Sarah a cup.

"White, no sugar. I hope that's right."

"Thanks." She gave him a quick smile and turned back to the doctor. "We drove him into town, so we've both had recent contact, and then this morning Melissa Gilbert drove him from Plenty River Station to Mulga Downs. He mixed with lots of people last night of course."

"What happened last night?" Dr Kumar's eyebrows lifted interrogatively. She paused in her note-taking.

"Friends of ours had just returned from their honeymoon in New York, and hosted a barbecue."

"New York—okay. Did they go to any other countries?"

"No, just the United States and even then, just the main tourist attractions. You don't think they could have brought back an infection, do you?"

"Right now, I don't know anything," Dr Kumar replied. "We have to keep an open mind and consider all possibilities. The blood tests may tell us more." She hooked the notes and clipboard back onto the end of the bed and turned to face them.

"Because of the severity of his symptoms, I will start a course of antibiotics straight away. We'll adjust treatment when the test results are back. In the meantime, check if anyone else is feeling unwell, and as a precaution, stay away from crowded public places in the interim. We don't want any infection spread throughout the town. In particular, limit your contact with children, the elderly and pregnant women."

Dr Kumar initiated the treatment she had outlined, and made arrangements for Chris to be moved to a private room in a ward on another floor. Joel brought in Chris's overnight bag from the car, and after that, there wasn't much that they could do.

"I'll take you home now," Sarah said to Joel. "I might return later to see if there's any news. I'd better call Kathy and let her know what's happened. Mark will be anxious as well."

Chris was now breathing with the aid of an oxygen mask. She squeezed his hand.

"I'll be back soon Chris. We've brought your bag in but if there is anything that you need, I can sort that out for you. Is there anyone I should call?"

There was only a grunt from beneath the mask, which she took to be a 'no'. His eyes seemed to focus on her so hopefully he understood what she'd said. Sarah turned at the door to look back at him. Her friend, who normally had such a substantial physical presence, looked suddenly frailer and smaller.

~*~

"Come in for a proper coffee. It will be better than that hospital brew, I promise." The look Joel gave her was inviting.

"That sounds like an offer too good to refuse."

Sarah was tired after the drive back to town, and pleased to have the opportunity to relax for a while. Still, she couldn't stay too long. She flung her bag and keys down on the coffee table while Joel busied himself in the kitchen. It gave her a chance to look around. You could learn a lot about a person from their possessions and sense of style.

The photo stood out because it was obviously something Joel had bought with him. It was framed, and sitting on a book shelf. No other photos were on display, so it must have been of some importance.

A young woman with her arm around a small child smiled at the camera. The physical similarities between the pair were strong enough that Sarah assumed them to be mother and child. She itched to pick the frame up to examine the picture closely. She glanced at Joel covertly but he was occupied with the coffee. She only had time to note that the woman was attractive, and the nature of her smile indicated a level of intimacy with the person behind the camera. Who was she? What was her relationship to Joel? Her curiosity was piqued. It made her think. Chris had been right with the questions he'd asked.

"Hope the milk is still okay. I bought it a couple of days ago but it should still be fresh. Make yourself comfortable." Joel handed her a mug.

Sarah sniffed at the aroma rising from the coffee. "Smells fine to me."

She perched on the edge of the lounge chair, with a half-smile in Joel's direction. He'd looked very at home in his kitchen and that was reassuring. She liked a man who not only looked good but was competent as well. So far, Joel ticked some of the boxes. Her thoughts wondered idly as to how well he would score in other areas. *Focus, Sarah. Drink your coffee.*

"Chris didn't look at all good by the time he was admitted," Joel said. "That was such a rapid decline. I've never quite seen anything like it, but my exposure to serious illness has been limited." He paused while taking a sip of his coffee. "I know you're good mates, but watching you both this afternoon, you're obviously very close to him."

There was a speculative tone to this comment.

"Chris has been good to me in the past. There have been times when I've needed support and he's always been there for me. I'm only returning the favour." She lowered her mug and glanced towards the window and the view outside while she thought about what she had said. "No, it's not *just* that. It's not a case of returning favours. When a good friend needs your help, you step up anyway."

"Yes, of course."

"I'm puzzled about what the problem might be," she continued. "I feel okay, don't you? I'm not planning on going to crowded places in the next couple of days but I hope we find out soon. Lucky we don't have exposure to any children." She glanced quickly at the photo.

"Well—not here, anyway."

He didn't elaborate. *Not here—then where?* His eyes met hers. Their mesmerising hue entranced her. You could swim in pools like that. Sarah looked away again, not wanting to make a fool of herself by looking for anything that wasn't there.

She cast around for what to say next. "What did you think of your station experience? Did you get some useful research material, besides lining up Rose for an interview?"

"Absolutely. Overall, it was very productive."

She might have imagined it, but Sarah thought that he was relieved at the change in topic.

There was a moment's strained silence. He put down his cup and took her hand in his. "Sarah, I can be a little dense at times but I can't help noticing you've been reserved with me today. I assume that how we left things last night has something to do with that. I…"

"It's okay," Sarah interrupted. "I wasn't exactly comfortable myself in taking things further. I guess we were carried away with the night and the atmosphere and all of that."

"There was more to it than just the atmosphere. I find you a very attractive woman. Surely you know that? I'm in no hurry. I'd like to savour every moment, particularly when it comes to you. I should probably explain there are a few things going on in my life right now, so there's a lot for me to focus on. If I seem distracted sometimes, it's because I'm not always good at compartmentalising things. That doesn't have any bearing on how I might feel about you."

Great. Now I'm a conflicting distraction. Is that woman part of what's going on? "Joel, you don't have to explain. I'm familiar with turmoil, and I'm in no hurry to complicate matters either."

"I don't want to pry," he said, "but from what I've picked up you've had more than your fair share of sadness to deal with." He grinned. "You've got some good friends there who obviously care deeply about you. In that regard, you're very lucky."

"Put like that, I suppose I am. Sweet as they are, I'm quite capable of looking after myself." She retrieved her hand from his grasp and stood up. "Thanks for the coffee. I'll leave you to sort out the rest of your weekend before it's over. I've got a few phone calls to make."

"Thank *you* for inviting me to join you on the trip to Mulga. I enjoyed meeting your friends. I hope Chris recovers soon." He pulled her close to him, and brushed her forehead with a feather-light kiss, his hands gently kneading her shoulders.

"O-o-oh—that feels so good. The drive back to town left its mark." With a soft sigh of release, she relaxed against him as his fingers worked their magic on the aching muscles. A man of many talents. Good coffee *and* strong fingers. What more could a girl want? A lot more if she was honest, but for now, this was fine. She straightened up, bracing herself with her hands against his chest to look up at him. "If you can keep that up on a regular basis, you and your legs will be fine. I'll call the hounds off."

He laughed. "I'll call you—okay? We can catch up for a meal through the week. You can introduce me to some of the prime eating establishments in town."

"Sounds like a plan. I'll put some thought into what gastronomic delights we can explore."

This time, his lips moved lower and he claimed hers with a kiss that was tantalising, but with more promise than passion. It was enough to ignite a slow burn in the pit of her belly and when he released her from the embrace, she was both regretful that there was not more, and reassured that the kindled response was not hers alone.

The call had been picked up on the second ring, which was some achievement given the size of the Mulga Downs homestead. Sarah tucked the handset under her chin, at the same time throwing the contents of her overnight bag onto her bed, sorting out what needed to be washed. She would only get through the weekend chores with some multi-tasking.

"Kathy? I wanted to give you an update on Chris."

"Great—we've been wondering. Everyone else has left now but I promised to keep people posted. Melissa was especially worried. I think he gave her rather a scare when his condition deteriorated so quickly. She's driven back to Plenty River, so I'll give the station a call."

"Well, he's still not good, but was admitted to hospital. When I dropped in half an hour ago, he was sleeping. There's no indication as yet on the cause of the problem, but they'll be running a battery of tests. I hope there'll be some news in a day or so. In the meantime, he's under observation."

"Nobody else has shown signs of coming down with anything, so it can't be something that he ate—not here anyway."

"They'll check that out at the hospital. The doctor asked us all sorts of questions—where he'd been, what he'd been doing, who he'd been with—that sort of thing. She wanted to know if he'd travelled overseas recently. He hasn't of course, but you have. Do you think you or Alex could have picked up an infection and brought it back with you?"

"Us? Infection? You're joking aren't you?" Kathy sounded incredulous.

"Well, she did ask us where you'd been, you know, what countries. Sorry Kathy but I had to tell her. I wouldn't think New York was a hot bed of infection though. Maybe something on the plane? You know people always talk about getting sick after being couped up in a plane with a long haul flight. Perhaps another passenger had Spanish Flu or Mexican Flu or some other unidentified American flu."

"Bubonic Plague perhaps?" Kathy laughed at her own comment, then was silent for a moment before continuing. "Neither of us is sick. We're fine; at least I think we are. Alex is out in the ute, but he was okay when he left."

"That's reassuring."

"You realise that I'm going to feel twitchy now. I'll be taking my temperature and looking in the mirror every five minutes. Who knows how many other people we've infected!"

Her tone changed. "Poor Chris. I feel awful. I hope they find out what it is soon. Perhaps there's a vaccination we can all get."

"It's too soon to start panicking. Why don't we wait until the hospital gets the results back for their tests? They took blood samples so testing will be underway, or when the lab staff get to work in the morning it will. I'll let you know as soon as I hear anything. I'll drop in at the hospital on my way to work tomorrow."

A sigh came down the phone line. "Thanks Sarah. I'd appreciate that. I think Mark is over at Jinka Station. He's mustering there all this coming week and he flew over there this afternoon to get set up and ready for the start in the morning. We'd better let him know as well."

"That's okay," said Sarah. "I'll ring Jinka. I'm sure they'll pass on the message. Thank Rose again for the wonderful hospitality. Joel sends his appreciation as well. He really enjoyed the experience, and meeting both of you of course. I'll call you in the morning."

No sooner had she disconnected from her conversation with Kathy, than the phone rang. It was Mark, looking for an update on Chris's condition.

"Hey Sugar, I thought you'd be home by now. What's the news on my old mate? Is he improving? He should know better than to give us a scare like that."

He was alarmed when Sarah told him about the trip back into town, but was relieved on learning the hospital had admitted him.

"What about you, Mark? How are you feeling?"

"I'm fine—fighting fit in fact. I'll feel much better when we know what the problem is with Chris; beyond piking of course."

"I'll tell him you said that. What sort of mate are you?"

He laughed. "Nothing I wouldn't say to his face, or he to mine for that matter."

They were good mates, that was true. She knew his glib remark hid his true feelings.

"I'll call in the morning and leave a message with Tom at the homestead. I'll let Kathy know as well so if there's any communication breakdown, give Kathy a call. Oh, and don't call me Sugar."

"Okay, Curly."

Sarah replaced the handset with exasperation. She ran her fingers through her tangled mane. Her hair was gritty with road dust and felt gross. It exacerbated her current mood. Respect; that was what she needed from those two—a little respect. Anyone would think she was a Kewpie Doll. Curly, and Sugar—what sort of names were those? Not names for someone who was appealing and what did Joel say? Attractive, that was it. She was an attractive woman. It was a long time since she had thought of herself in that way, and equally as long since she had behaved as though she was. Time for a change.

The chirpy tones of Radio Alice woke her the next morning, with cheerful banter from the announcer, interspersed with sound bites of news.

Does anyone listen to that drivel in the morning? I need something gentle and soothing to ease me into Monday morning. Must speak to Joel about that. She wondered briefly if she could claim a day off on the grounds the doctor had recommended she stay away from crowded places. It probably wouldn't wash with the boss. She didn't have extensive contact with the general public and not with children. Just the childish. She pushed herself out the door earlier than usual so she could swing past the hospital, grabbing a banana to eat on the way.

At first she thought that the notice on the door of Chris's room referred to a previous occupant. On reflection, it hadn't been there the night before. It also carried the day's date. It

93

declared the room to be an infection zone, and no visitors were to enter without reporting to the ward desk. She retraced her steps down the passage.

"Excuse me?"

The ward sister didn't look up until she had finished writing something in a file. She looked slightly annoyed. "Visiting hours aren't until 10:00. You'll have to come back later."

"But I'm just on my way to work. I only wanted an update on Chris Harris's condition."

"Are you a relative?"

"No, I'm a close friend."

"I'm sorry. I can't discuss a patient's condition with you."

"But…we're like family. I brought him in for treatment last night." Sarah struggled to contain her rising irritation. She knew that nothing would be achieved by losing her temper, but really—some hospital protocols were too stupid for words. The sound of footsteps signalled the approach of someone else. Dr Kumar.

"Dr Kumar—Good morning! Do you remember me? I brought Chris Harris in last night. I wanted to check on him before going to work today, but there is a notice stuck to his door. Can I see him?"

"You can see him briefly, but you must wear a mask and no physical contact is permitted. We don't have test results back yet and his condition has not improved. We need to take every precaution until we have more definitive information. How are you feeling? Any temperature increase; aches and pains?"

"No, I'm fine—really."

"It might be advisable if you stay away from work until we know more. Leave your phone number with the ward sister and we'll call you when the test results are available. It might not be today, or even tomorrow. Depends on what it is. The sister will also give you a mask. Disinfect your hands before entering that room.”

The doctor was brusque and still looked tired. She entered another room, leaving Sarah hovering at the desk. After asking for the mask as instructed and leaving her phone number, she walked back down the passage and gingerly opened the door to Chris's room. The lighting was dim, presumably for his comfort. Chris was awake, and his eyes widened when he saw Sarah behind the face mask.

“How are you feeling?” she asked quietly, then grimaced. Stupid question. “Sorry about the mask. They don't think it's a good idea if I introduce any germs at this stage.”

She tried to downplay the fact that he was the one who was infectious.

He gave her a thumbs-up. “Just slightly tired, that's all. I only need some rest and I'll be out of here in no time. I've heaps of work on at the moment. Can't leave it all to Mark.” His voice sounded hoarse. He closed his eyes and seemed to be breathing with effort.

“Oh, I don't know—might do him good to have to put in a good day's work for a change. If I were you, I'd stay here a while longer. It'll make him appreciate you all the more.”

“I like your thinking; I might just do that.” His eyes closed and after watching him for a time, Sarah decided that he must have drifted off to sleep. His face was flushed, contrasting with the white of the hospital sheets, and his skin looked taut and dry. How could this have happened so quickly?

Tight bands of fear wrapped themselves around her. She couldn't stand to lose somebody else she cared about dearly. The loss was never far from her thoughts. Not trusting herself to hide the tears that hovered, she turned for the door.

“You'll come back again?” The whisper was barely audible.

With her hand on the door handle, she looked back at the figure on the bed. "Of course; I'll be back as soon as I can."

The radio blared into action as she started the car. *Joel is probably at work already. I'll update him about what the doctor said.* Sarah drove past his apartment in case he was still there but the driveway was empty. She wondered again about the photo she had seen the day before. That woman had been so pretty. What did she mean to Joel? How could she find out without seeming to pry?

On cue, his voice emerged from the car radio, delivering a station promo. He sounded so smooth, with a voice like chocolate velvet. Wow! She could really fall for a voice like that.

Once back home, she rang work, letting them know she wouldn't be in the office on doctor's orders but that she was perfectly fine. Staying home was a precautionary measure until Chris's test results were returned. She arranged for some documents to be delivered to her so she could continue working on some monthly reports, and stressed that if there were any queries, the office shouldn't hesitate to ring her.

A quick call to Kathy provided the morning's update, and from there the outback network was going to spread the word. Kathy promised to call Mark as well.

Joel was next on Sarah's list. When she was put through from reception at the radio station, she gave him the latest information, including the recommendation that she should stay home for now.

"I guess that means you should be home as well," she continued. "We were in a contained environment with Chris on the drive back to town. We could both be at risk."

"You're right, but it's a chance I'll have to take. There is a lot on at the moment and at least the station runs with only a few hands. I'll be careful—wash my hands and keep my own coffee cup and not cough near anyone else. Do you think that will do it?"

"I'm not an expert on infection control, so this decision is up to you. It was just a recommendation from the doctor anyway, not a directive."

"That makes me feel slightly better. At least, it can't apply to us seeing each other. We've both been exposed to any potential infection and so it won't matter if we're in close proximity."

There was a pause while she heard voices in the background and then a door slamming. It went quiet again. "Sorry about the interruption," he said. "Did I tell you I'm thinking of doing some massage training? If it makes you so pliant and relaxed, there could be all sorts of benefits."

"That sounds a wonderful idea, but Joel—you can massage my shoulders anytime. You don't need a certificate for that." She rolled her shoulders and eased the muscles, imagining those strong fingers working their magic.

"No. I seemed to do just fine without it."

Chapter 8

"THIS IS DOCTOR Kumar calling. Are you free to talk?"

"Yes, yes of course. Wait a second—I'll shut the office door to give me some privacy. ...Okay, go ahead. Do you know what's wrong with Chris?"

"Yes, we do. The results have just come in. He has Q Fever."

"Q Fever—what's that? Is it serious?"

"Yes and no. Untreated, the result can be extreme with a range of secondary impacts, but with the right antibiotics it's quite treatable. It's picked up by exposure to cattle or contaminated animal products, and it's a disease that is most commonly seen in abattoir workers. Didn't you say that he undertook cattle mustering as part of his job?"

"Yes. Mostly he's in the air but sometimes he lands close to the cattle or even camps out overnight."

"Well, he's been very unlucky. I don't see much of it. Most people who are at risk are vaccinated against it.

"Will there be any long-term effects?"

"He has a severe case, so could be off work for up to a month, but no—once he's fully recovered, he should be fine. It's fortunate you brought him to hospital as quickly as you did. We'll monitor him for residual muscle pain or any other side effects. I've amended his treatment accordingly and we should see a positive response fairly soon."

The news was both a relief and confusing. Sarah had seen how quickly it evolved. "And what about those of us who've had contact with Chris? Are we likely to be infectious?"

"As it is only acquired from animals and not from humans, no—there won't be a risk to you. You can resume your normal activities."

"That's good to hear. Thank you for letting me know."

After replacing the handset, Sarah sat for a while, contemplating the news. It was great there were some answers but even so, the news wasn't brilliant for Chris. He'd be so upset at being off work for that long. Who would have thought of Q Fever? She would make sure to spread the word about the need for vaccination. Chris was lucky he'd received medical care without too much delay. If he'd been at some remote location on his own, it might have been a different story.

It was an excuse for a celebration. She needed to call Joel anyway to give him the news. She could invite him to dinner. At her place. She picked up the phone to call him before she got cold feet. It was so long since she'd entertained anyone, especially with a cooked meal. Not since Dave.

She was about to hang up, when he answered. Not off the hook then. She took a breath, twiddling one of her side curls as she spoke. "Hi Joel, Sarah here. The good news is Chris has his diagnosis and it's not infectious for us. You're not a danger. You can fraternize with whoever you want."

"That's a relief." A note of puzzlement crept into his voice. "Is there bad news as well?"

"No, at least, I hope not. I thought you might like to come around for dinner tonight. We can celebrate, and I'll explain to you then all about Q Fever. That's what Chris has. It's not good news for him but could be a lot worse.

"Thank you, I'd like that. Both the dinner and learning more. Is seven a reasonable time?"

With arrangements finalised, Sarah disconnected the call, aware that she'd reached another milestone.

She buried her face in the red blooms and inhaled deeply.

"They smell divine. How did you know I loved roses and how did you find any that had some scent?" Sarah rummaged in a cupboard for a vase while Joel took off his jacket and slung it over the arm of the sofa.

"I may not have been in town long, but even I've established some contacts. Need great-smelling flowers? I'm your man. Need a car repairer who asks no questions? I'm your man. Need a forged passport? I'm your man. Need a hit man? I'm your man."

"What did you just say?"

He roared with laughter. "You should see your face. I'm joking, Sarah, I'm joking. The florist advertises with the station. I have no idea where to find a hit man and doubt I would ever want to."

"I'm not sure whether to be relieved or disappointed. Still, if I need to make somebody disappear, I'll do it myself rather than outsource. It's not right to ask somebody else to do your dirty work."

"I couldn't agree more." He'd brought a cooler bag with him and he now unzipped it to rummage inside. "I'm glad you weren't in a disappearing frame of mind last time I was here. I might never have been seen again and no one would have known where look. Shall I open this?" He proffered a bottle of Yellow Glen that he'd taken from his bag.

"Bubbles as well! You're a darling. Of course, you should open it. Just aim it away from me. Dinner's under control but still needs some oven time so we can sit down and enjoy a drink while we wait."

She felt remarkably relaxed. She'd not forgotten anything crucial at the supermarket, she'd arrived home from work with enough time to get everything prepared, the flat was presentable and she'd had time for a leisurely shower. She'd even made sure her bed was made with fresh sheets and the bedroom was looking tidier than it had that morning.

The challenging issue had been deciding what to wear. Casual chic was the look she had in mind, but it was not a concept that came easily to her. Casual, yes; chic, more of a challenge. With curly hair that had a stubborn mind of its own, she settled for drawing one side back with a comb so at least part of her face was free from bubbly corkscrews. She considered a little black dress, but that suggested a formality which didn't fit the occasion. A red dress was discarded for being too suggestive. In the end, she abandoned the dress idea altogether and settled on black trousers, topped by an over-blouse of metallic blues and greens.

Her freckles would never be vanquished, particularly living in a location like Alice Springs but at least they were toned down with a light dusting of powder. The rest of her make-up was subtle, with the intention to enhance rather than exaggerate. Normally, she padded bare feet around the flat, but on this occasion she chose a pair of simple black sandals. They were new, but comfortable, and contributed to the overall look she sought. The bracelet Kathy brought back from New York and a light spray of perfume provided the finishing touches.

Ordinarily, she would have been all butterflies at extending a dinner invitation, but something had changed. She wasn't sure if it was seeing the photo on Joel's bookshelf or the conversation that had followed that afternoon, but she was happy now to let the relationship evolve at its own pace. She wasn't even certain that she could classify it as a relationship.

Sure, Joel had stirred feelings and emotions she had thought were dead and buried with Dave Bishop, but knowing they could be resurrected was enough for now. The pressure was off and the best thing was—she was the one who had released it. In the words of Doris Day, '*Que sera, sera*'. Whatever would be would be. Perhaps she needed this connection with Joel to dispel the ghosts of the past.

Sarah indicated Joel should sit on the sofa. She pressed play on her new CD player and light easy-listening music filled the room. She took the opposite end of the sofa, slipping her shoes off and curling one leg beneath her as she swivelled to face him.

"Cheers." She raised her glass in salute.

"Here's to us," he responded, raising his glass in return.

There was a momentary pause. Sarah cast around for an opening topic. "You must be starting to feel at home in Alice. It won't be long before friends and family start finding excuses to visit. That's what usually happens. So many people mean to visit the Centre but never get around to it until they have a valid excuse like visiting a local resident. Are you expecting any visitors in the near future?"

"There are no defined plans."

"Are your parents still working? That will probably limit the time they have for travelling to their annual leave."

"Yes they are. There aren't any immediate plans, or if there are, nobody's told me about them."

"But aren't they interested to see where you're living and working?"

"I'm sure they are, and they'll probably come at some stage, but not just yet. It's complicated."

What's complicated about family visiting? Sarah was puzzled at the stilted path the conversation took, but the unspoken message came across loud and clear. It was a conversation Joel didn't want to have. She remembered she wanted to talk to him about the radio station's choice of music in the mornings, and moved the discussion onto safer topics.

"That reminds me. I've been meaning to talk to you about the morning radio program."

"Really? What about it?" Joel sat up a little straighter, looking mildly surprised.

"Don't you think that breakfast duo is just a little too chirpy and well—infantile comes to mind but that's not quite the word. The rubbish they go on with makes my head ache and first thing in the morning, and that's not what I want. I need something calming and soothing to ease me into the day."

"They're supposed to wake you up and get you up and at 'em, not let you drift back to sleep in a comfy cocoon. Sounds like they succeeded."

"Those two slam me into the day," she protested. "I start my morning with a headache, and that I have to tell you is not good. Surely there can be a mix of music and some halfway intelligent discussion and interviews?"

She gave him a range of suggestions which he politely promised to consider, warning her they had to take all opinions into account.

"It's not all my say you know. We do market surveys to see what the listening public wants and then of course we wouldn't exist without our sponsors. Management and the national marketing team have their input as well. I'll pass the word along that a submission has been made by a high profile representative of the local community."

She reached out a foot and poked him on the thigh with a toe. "Now you're taking the mickey. C'mon—I think our dinner's ready."

The meal was everything Sarah had hoped. The fish was moist and tender, flaking gently under the fork. The asparagus spears were still al dente and bathed but not drowned in the Hollandaise sauce. The Hasselback potatoes were cooked to a crisp finish and perfectly fanned and the salad was topped with cherry tomatoes that tantalised with their sweetness.

The strawberries in champagne jelly had been given just enough time to set in the fridge before being lightly drizzled in cream, topped with a couple of mint leaves and a shaving of chocolate. She placed them on the table with a flourish. Joel was suitably impressed. And so he should have been. It was a damn good effort.

"Coffee? We could take it outside on the veranda. I'll light a mosquito coil to keep the bugs at bay."

"Sounds good on both counts. Where do you keep the coils? I'll get one going while you address the coffee. That way I can both feel useful *and* get to play with a little fire."

Sarah rolled her eyes in mock tease. "There's something about the naked flame that kindles the caveman in even the mildest man." She pointed outside. "Go for it. The coils and the matches live on top of the electricity meter box. That way there's always a coil close handy when I need one."

While Joel organised the coils, Sarah made the coffee, and loaded the coffee pot and the cups onto a tray. The aromatic smoke from the mosquito coil was curling around the chairs by the time she backed into the screen door to push it open, her hands grasping the handles of the tray.

"I think the dishes can wait until the morning," Sarah said.

"You won't have any argument from me. I'm sure they'll keep."

It was a pleasant night and fortunately the other occupants of the adjoining company flats were not in evidence. Sarah had no desire for prying eyes. Although happy to share barbecues and night caps at other times, this evening belonged to her and Joel alone. They sat on the veranda furniture, the coffee tray on a lowset table between them. She handed Joel a cup of coffee, indicating the milk and sugar on the tray.

"Thank you. No sugar—I'm sweet enough, in case you hadn't noticed."

She flicked him a quick smile of acknowledgement. The crickets serenaded them with their evening song, and for a while they sat in companionable silence, broken only by the flapping of the moths as they threw themselves against the veranda light. The night air gently embraced them. The outdoor lights cocooned them from the dark, though the moonlight scantily outlined the things that sat out of the circle of light. They sat in their own private world, with a silhouetted hint of what lay beyond. Sarah could feel the easing of the stress and tension of the last couple of days.

She picked up her cup and looked in Joel's direction. "I can't believe how unlucky Chris has been. It's good he now has a definitive diagnosis. I imagined all sorts of dreadful things. Not that Q Fever isn't bad of course. I thought Alex and Kathy must have brought back some weird infection they'd picked up on their travels."

"I had some of the same thoughts," Joel said.

"Instead, it's a weird infection he picked up from the cattle. I've not heard much about it before and certainly not met anyone who has fallen ill with the disease. We'll all know about it from now on though."

Joel added the milk to his coffee, stirring it until the milky whorls blended to a homogenous deep tan. "It's not exactly a city disease, so I've a big knowledge gap as well. How is he feeling now?"

"I didn't see him this evening as there wasn't enough time after work, but he looked much better this morning. The antibiotics must be working their magic."

"You're pretty fond of Chris."

It was a flat statement.

"Of course, I am. Like I told you, he's been a good mate."

"A good mate… are you sure that's all it is? From his side I mean. I get the impression his interest might be a little more than that. He's very protective. I'm thinking of his comments out at Mulga Downs."

Where was this going? Sarah looked at him closely but his expression remained enigmatic. "That's crazy. Chris doesn't have any interest in me, beyond what you see."

"But I do see."

"See what? What are you talking about?" Her look was one of confusion and there was a subtle change in atmosphere.

Joel looked away from her before answering. "I know you're a very caring person but the amount of time you've spent visiting Chris in the past couple of days seems to go above the call of duty. Are you sure you're being honest with yourself and with me?" He sat forward in his chair, looking at her intently. "Sarah, I don't want to get caught up in a messy triangle. That's the last thing I need in my life right now."

His expression was more earnest than it had been. "I don't want to bore you with past experiences – we've all had those – but three's a crowd in my view."

"Joel, you're seeing complications where none exist."

Where had all this come from? She tried to repress her exasperation. He couldn't think visiting Chris on her way to and from work was unreasonable, surely? It wasn't as if Chris had anyone else in Alice to look out for him and what else were mates supposed to do?

"We've been good friends for a long time. Chris has been there for me in the past when times were grim. I'm just stepping up the mark now and pleased to do so."

He looked at her speculatively, carefully placing his cup back on the saucer. There was deliberateness to this action. Watching it, bands of tension tightened around Sarah's chest. She lifted her eyes from the cup back to his face, but his expression was unreadable. The veranda light was not very strong and soft shadows crept from the outer reaches, casting a mysterious definition to the contours of his face. The chiselled outlines to his jaw indicated a strength she hadn't perceived before.

Unexpectedly he smiled, and reached out to take her hand. "Of course, knowing you as I'm learning to do, I wouldn't have expected you to be any less caring. I just want you to keep your eyes wide open and to stay honest with me."

"But wouldn't you…"

A harsh ringing erupted from Joel's bag, disturbing the ambience of the night. He was the only person she knew who had one of the new mobile phones and it now rang with a discordant sound. The mood had already changed though.

"Sorry. I wasn't expecting a call." He scrabbled for the handset, and stepped out into the pseudo privacy of the night. He had his back to her, but Sarah could hear the conversation clearly. What was so important it couldn't wait until the morning?

"Hello?… Miguel… do you know what time it is?… What's the matter?… Calm down; I'll deal with it, okay?…Look, I can't talk about this now. I'll call you when I get home."

While this was happening, she turned over what he had just said. Honesty? Did he think she wasn't being honest with him? Should she have told him about Dave? There was no reason not to except Dave belonged to a part of her that was private. With the anniversary approaching, she wanted to keep Dave and her memories to herself. That wasn't dishonest, surely?

Joel disconnected his call and turned back to where Sarah still sat.

"Is there a problem?" she asked.

"Just a personal issue. It's nothing to worry about."

Didn't sound like nothing to me, and who's Miguel?

His silence made it evident she wasn't going to be told.

He stood in front of her, momentarily blocking the light. "Sarah, it's been a wonderful evening and I really enjoyed it. I should call it a day though. I've an early start in the morning." Joel reached out and in one fluid movement, pulled her to her feet and into his arms.

"Don't change Sarah," he whispered into her hair. "Don't change from the caring, funny, adorable person you are. Just be careful, that's all."

Why does everyone tell me to be careful of everyone else? She braced her hands against his chest so that she could look up at him. *Do I really look so ditzy that I can't look after myself?*

The kiss they exchanged had a sense of the obligatory rather than the passionate, leaving her confused and saddened. The evening had started so well. There was the nagging feeling that if it weren't for that phone call, it might have finished differently. She surveyed her pristine bedroom with irony some time later. Why had she bothered? As she turned out the lights before going to bed, the scent of the roses hung heavily on the air.

Once his fever was under control, Chris's condition quickly stabilised. The antibiotics were doing their job. Dr Kumar gave him the all-clear to leave hospital on the proviso he came back at a specified time for review and follow-up blood tests. Sarah picked him up in her lunch hour and delivered him back to his apartment.

"How are you off for groceries? Do you need any shopping done? We can stop off at the mini-mart on the way home."

"Thanks Curly. If we pick up some fresh bread, milk and eggs, that will be good. I don't have much of an appetite at the moment."

"Okay—your wish is my command."

"Wish it was," he muttered under his breath.

"What?"

"I said it was good to be out. I've had enough of hospitals for a while."

Sarah gave him a puzzled look but didn't pursue the matter.

"So… anything exciting happen in the world while I've been incommunicado?"

"Not really—just the usual. I've kept those who need to know informed of your progress. Joel and I were semi-quarantined for a while until your diagnosis was confirmed but that didn't last long. I did some work from home during that period."

"So you haven't caught up with him since the weekend then?"

"Oh yes—we had dinner together mid-week. I cooked, which is a change for me and I've not heard of any after effects, so I assume he survived." She looked away from the road briefly. "Did you know Joel has one of those new mobile phones? I think it came with the job. It rang just before he left. I hadn't seen one before."

"Is that so? He must be important to have one of those. I heard they cost a mint. Why would someone need to call him at night?"

"I've no idea. It was someone called Miguel."

"Miguel—what sort of name is that? Are you sure which team he bats for Curly? Getting late night calls from someone called Miguel makes you wonder."

Sarah took her eyes off the road long enough to throw him an exasperated look. "I think your stay in hospital has addled your brain. Anyway—it's Joel's business who he gets calls from."

As she drove away from depositing Chris and his groceries to his flat, she felt mildly annoyed with him. Why did he persist with such bigoted rubbish? What was wrong with the man? What really rankled though was that his suggestions prompted questions in her own mind. Had Joel really needed to go that night or had he just been making excuses? *Damn you Chris.*

She wanted to call Joel the following day. Now that Chris was out of hospital, the ad-hoc after work Friday gathering was a certainty. She'd slipped in to the hotel again recently and hadn't been challenged. It was a good opportunity to invite Joel too.

She reached for the phone a couple of times and then stopped, rehearsing in her mind what she would say. She chewed her lip uncertainly. Inviting him would serve two purposes. Firstly, she wanted to see him again and needed to reassure herself that things were fine between them. Secondly, their appearance together would be a public statement and perhaps it was time for that. If he declined the invitation, what would that tell her? It was a risk. She sighed. *Just do it.*

She rang the work number. He picked up straight away.

"Sarah—you got in first. I meant to call to say what a great dinner the other night. Sorry, things have been hectic since then. In fact, I'm about to rush out the door now."

"I know you're busy, so I won't keep you. I wanted to ask if you'd like to join the usual mob of reprobates at the Hotel Alice this Friday night. It's the end-of-week thing and you'll know some of the people who are likely to wander in."

"Normally I would, but I won't be here. Sorry Sarah, but I'll be in Melbourne. Just off to the airport now. If we can take a rain check on that I'd love to join you another time."

"I didn't realise you were going away." *He hasn't mentioned anything about this before. Why is he going again?*

"Something came up at short notice. I've got to go, but I'll give you a call when I get back. I'm not quite sure when that will be."

"Oh…okay…have a safe trip then. I hope you sort everything out."

She stared at the phone after disconnecting the call. It was a business-like conversation, which was understandable, she reasoned. He was at work after all, and who knew who else could have been listening in at the other end. Still, did it reflect the fact that his interest in her wasn't so strong after all? He was a man with secrets, and that made her uncomfortable. What was he hiding? The conversations she'd had with both Chris and Kathy came back to haunt her.

She stewed on this for a while, before slipping out of the office, heading into the local coffee shop and ordering herself a double-shot brew. *Time to wise up girl,* she told herself resolutely. *You've hung your hat on a star that simply isn't going to shine. It's too soon anyway and the last thing you need is a dud relationship to complicate things. Your life is fine as it is.*

Chapter 9

"TWO YEARS! TWO whole years! It seems like yesterday."

Her voice was hoarse, reflecting the emotion of the moment. They stood, arms slung around each other's shoulders, staring at the headstone. Dave's sister, Meryl had joined Sarah to mark the anniversary. Her eyelashes clumped with un-leashed tears. She turned to face Sarah.

"We'll always be friends, won't we? I was so looking forward to you being my sister-in-law, and you were already one of the family. I'd hate it if we didn't stay friends. I could kill that brother of mine for not sticking around."

Sarah struggled to contain her own tears. She'd told herself she wasn't going to cry today. In the past year, she'd cried enough to flood the Todd River. "Of course we'll be friends—we *are* friends."

That did it. First one quivering drop and then the other slid down her face. The struggle to retain her composure was doomed. Her face contorted as a wave of grief swamped her. She buried her face in Meryl's shoulder, leaving wet patches on the other woman's shirt.

"Oh sweetie, it was so not fair. Sorry, I shouldn't have said I would kill him."

Her own tears now falling in sympathy, Meryl hugged Sarah tight. They rocked side to side clamped together until they both developed the sniffles and had to release each other to search for dry tissues in their bags. It was at that point, Sarah—face still red and blotchy—started to giggle.

"Can you imagine what he'd be thinking right now? He'd be saying, *What a pair of wet blankets! You two turn on the waterworks at the drop of a hat.*"

"He'd be right too," Meryl agreed, blowing her nose. "Not without due cause, mind you. I don't know about you but I could do with a drink. Time to bid my brother farewell for now. Let's clear out of here."

Over a shared meal at the local Chinese restaurant, and sustained with a bottle of sparkling wine, they caught up on recent news.

"Here's to Dave," said Meryl as they clinked glasses, "and here's to us, the two most fabulous women he was privileged to know."

The wine tasted good, and the company was even better.

Sarah hadn't seen Meryl for months. She had missed that easy camaraderie with someone who knew and understood the history of her relationship with Dave. They could talk about things other people wouldn't understand. They could also have a drink while doing it.

Meryl topped up Sarah's glass.

"So, what's new in your life? Is there anyone special?"

"Not really." The small sigh and dropped gaze was a giveaway.

"Hey, this is me you're talking to. Why do I get the feeling there's something you're not telling me?"

"Well, there is–*was*—someone, but I've decided it's all too hard. I don't think I'm ready, aside from any other issues."

Meryl placed the bottle back in the ice bucket, and elbows on the table, rested her chin on her interlaced fingers. It was a stance of interrogation. "Who is he and how did you meet?"

Sarah gave a brief history of her association with Joel, leading up to their last discussion. "I don't think he's really interested, and anyway—it's probably too soon."

Meryl reached across the table and took Sarah's hand. "Sarah, it's been a year. I know that time's gone quickly, but Dave didn't want you to immerse yourself in mourning forever. I heard him say as much. It's time to move on. You need to be ready of course, and there'll never quite be anyone like Dave. There'll be someone else though who is also special in his own way. Don't shut yourself off from the possibility."

Sarah didn't respond immediately. She thought of that last conversation before Dave slid into his final sleep. He'd said what she hadn't wanted to hear; that she should make a new life for herself; that she had a right to be happy.

She was embarrassed when two tears slid down her face. She'd thought she was done with weeping and dabbed furiously at her face with the napkin.

"I'm fine—really. It's the drink. Too much champagne makes me maudlin."

With her head on one side, Meryl gave a sad, conciliatory smile. "Sure, it does. Just remember—live your life as Dave wanted you to. You owe him that and you owe it to yourself. It's time to move on."

Meryl's words stuck with Sarah, but if anything, they pulled her down emotionally. Her thoughts tumbled in all directions as she reassessed her life.

It's time. You need to take back control of your life. She knew what she'd told herself the day before, but her life wasn't fine. Dave was gone, and nothing was going to change that.

Seeing Kathy and Alex so happy had stirred memories and emotions. She was always the bridesmaid, never the bride and at this rate she probably never would be.

It was easy to understand why Joel had suddenly appeared desirable. She'd pinned her hopes on him. It wasn't Joel's fault she'd tried to fill a hole in her heart. She'd probably been a little too obvious. Thinking about that now was embarrassing. She'd been such a fool.

She sat at the table with a piece of paper in front of her. Time to draw up a plan. Did she want to stay in Alice? What else might she do? Perhaps a career change was in order.

She made some notes detailing her options. She'd not done much travelling and perhaps it was time she did. Some suggestions she underlined and others she crossed out. The more she looked at it, the more confused she became.

Abandoning the task, she grabbed a cold drink from the fridge and sauntered outside to the veranda. She stretched in the fresh air, easing a cramp in her shoulders. Someone else from the complex had left a copy of the *Centralian Advocate* on the outdoor table. She picked it up and leafed through, happy to have the diversion.

It was the picture that caught her eye. A couple in mid swirl, her skirt flaring, his arm flung in the air, and their pose one of dramatic intensity. The local community college was running classes on flamenco dancing. It looked fun. She scanned the details. The term was about to start and a class was being held the following Monday evening. She didn't need to think long about it. *I'm in. Time for the new me. I might even learn Spanish as well.* A decision—any decision—was welcome. *New life, here I come.*

Sarah heard the music before she reached the door. It was full of fiery passion and foot-tapping rhythm. She hesitated outside, now uncertain. She didn't have a partner. What had made her think this was a good idea?

She turned to bolt and bumped into someone who approached the venue from behind her. She hadn't heard his footsteps over the music.

A man reached out to steady her as she nearly lost her balance. His black shirt was slashed in a deep vee down the front, showing his chiselled chest, and a brilliant red cummerbund topped his tight trousers. A heavy gold chain nestled in the dark hairs exposed on his torso. "Hey, senorita! Not leaving already?"

"I'm sorry; I didn't hear you. I don't think this is my class."

"And why not? Listen to ze music; doesn't it seize your 'eart, make you want to dance? In ze flamenco, you can truly express ze emotions."

"Yes, but…" How to explain the thought of expressing her emotions terrified her?

The man released her arms, and she took a step back, putting a protective distance between them. He was smiling at her, and judging by his outfit, he was an instructor in the course.

"Come, Senorita. Try my class. I promise you will enjoy learning ze dance."

With an arm around her shoulders, he swept her with him into the room where the early arrivals already waited. The guitarist sat in a corner of the room, running through his repertoire. Some students gathered in small groups, quietly chatting; others tapped their feet and swayed to the music. Any thoughts of escape were thwarted.

A dramatically attractive woman swept into the room. She wore a long dress, with a tight bodice and flared ruffled skirt. The red and black was the final give-away. She was the second half of the teaching duo.

116

Tomás introduced himself, his partner Maria, and the musician to the class. People in a mixture of age groups stood around. Some had come together, and they clung in their little cliques. Just like the first day at school. They all stared at the instructors curiously. Were they partners in life, or just in dance?

It didn't take Tomás long to change the atmosphere. He and Maria twirled in demonstration. Soon, everyone was up and stamping their way through the basic moves. The music was seductive. It enticed and lured you, beckoning with tantalising rhythm until it was impossible to stay still. Tomás mixed up the class, making partners change every so often. You never knew who you would be dancing with next.

Despite her initial reticence, Sarah enjoyed herself. Nobody knew her, nor her background. She wasn't the woman whose fiancé died. She was the woman losing herself in movement and dance, responding to the music and focussed on her dance partner.

At the end of the lesson, Tomás stood at the door as the class filed out. He clapped the men on the shoulder, his farewells a little more intimate with the women. Maria and the guitarist were talking in a corner of the room.

Tomás took Sarah's hand and kissed it, all the while looking up into her eyes. "Zank you, Senorita for being in my class. You will come again?"

He kept hold of her hand, gently moving his thumb in a circular motion over the back of it. He was flirting. She knew he would probably flirt with her eighty-year-old grandmother, but loved it all the same. *Tomás, you can flirt with me as much as you like. This girl's going to lap it up.* She licked her lips suggestively.

"Thank *you*, Tomás. Of course I'll be back. I can hardly wait." Perhaps she could try out her Spanish on him. At least, when she'd learnt some, she could.

She wondered what she had taken on when she sat in the classroom for the language lesson. Her classmates were a smattering of retirees exploring third age options, and young people looking for language survival skills before taking off for a gap year in Europe or South America. Sarah sat somewhere in the middle.

Looking around, she spotted another woman she knew vaguely from the gym. "Monica, Hi, or should I say 'Hola'. What are you doing here?"

"Same as you, I would think. Trying to learn Spanish. I learned some Italian at school, so I'm hoping that will give me a head start." Monica shrugged her shoulders in an open-handed gesture. "I'm planning some overseas travel and didn't feel like learning French, so here I am."

The two women sat together, comparing notes and answers. By the end of the first session, they were able to say, *Cual es tu nombre? Mi nombre es Sarah*, or *Mi nombre es Monica. Comó está?* It was a start. For homework, they had to learn the days of the week, and counting up to twenty.

"Want to catch up through the week?" asked Monica. "We can test each other and practice our vocabulary."

"That sounds a great idea. It'll ensure I do the homework, instead of getting side-tracked. We can grab a cheap and cheerful meal at the same time."

They finalised arrangements before heading for home. Sarah was quietly pleased with herself. Two new classes and a new friend. It was so long since she'd pushed herself, but her life was already changing.

"Uno, dos, tres, cuatro, cinco…"
"What are you muttering about, Curly?"

Sarah turned from hanging the washing on the line to find Chris standing there, hands on hips and a quizzical look on his face.

"I'm counting."

"Counting what? Didn't sound like anything I know."

"It's Spanish. Are you allowed out by yourself? You didn't drive here, did you?"

"No need to fuss; I'm fine. I didn't know you spoke Spanish."

She picked up the empty laundry basket. "I don't speak Spanish—I'm learning Spanish. There's a significant difference."

She led the way back to her flat, and after a moment's hesitation, Chris followed her.

"Take a seat on the veranda," she called over her shoulder. "I'll bring out a jug of iced tea."

She grabbed the jug and a couple of glasses, and when she came back to the veranda, Chris was sprawled in one of the outdoor chairs.

"Bored with your own company?" she asked. "You need to take up a hobby or a night class. I can recommend it."

He shook his head. "You never cease to amaze me, Curly. I thought you might need some company. Here I am thinking about Dave and wondering how you're coping, this being a significant time of year and all, and I find you yabbering in Spanish! I'm impressed. What brought this on?"

She poured them each a drink and pulled another chair up to the cane table. She didn't answer immediately, instead looking around at the garden and thinking how it must seem. She wasn't openly fretting about Dave, or wallowing in his memory, but was exploring new things. Would Chris think she didn't care? How to explain? Of course, in a way, Dave was behind it.

She pursed her lips with the effort of collecting her thoughts. "If you were thinking it's been a difficult time with the anniversary of Dave's death, you'd be right. It's something I'll never totally be over, but I know I have to live my life as he would have wanted. Meryl helped me to remember that. Did I tell you she was in town last week?"

"You didn't, but I saw her in the mall. I guessed Dave might have something to do with it."

Yeah—Dave's influence still touches us all. "We caught up over a meal and it was so good to see her again. Anyway, resulting from our conversation, I realised I've allowed myself to slide into a rut lately. It's time I explored new experiences and made a few plans for my future."

A look of alarm crossed Chris's face. The fingers of one hand drummed on the arm of the chair, and he looked pointedly at the brochures held down on the table by a garden rock.

"Plans? That sounds intriguing. You're not thinking of leaving, are you?"

"That was one of the options I considered," she admitted. "For now, I'm learning flamenco dancing on Monday nights and Spanish on Wednesday nights. I'm thinking about a trip to Spain though. Just a holiday, for now."

He looked visibly relieved and sat back again in his chair. "You had me going for a while there. I thought you were going to up and leave us. It wouldn't be the same around here without you." He looked at her with a smirk, head on one side. "Can anyone come and watch the classes? Do they dance on tables there?"

"Not funny." She threw a cushion at him, which he adeptly caught and wisely put out of reach.

"Sorry—couldn't resist that. I expect a ticket for your final performance though."

Sarah refreshed their glasses and they caught up on local news. Sarah called it gossip, but Chris was adamant it was nothing of the sort. Industry reconnaissance was his term of preference. He wasn't cleared to fly again, but declared himself significantly improved. He looked it as well.

"Are you coming down to the pub tonight, Curly? Mark's flying back to town and we're catching up with a few of the others at Hotel Alice."

"Thanks, but I might catch up with some homework. Give my regards to Mark. Don't get involved in any fights."

Chapter 10

THE KNOCK AT the door sounded impatient. Sarah wiped her hands on a towel before answering it. She squealed her delight.

"Kathy—you're back in town. It's so good to have another woman around again. Do you know how much I've missed you?"

The two women exchanged a hug with undisguised grins.

Well, you're going to see me more regularly from here on. I start back at StationAir on Monday. I've got a few errands to run over the weekend, but after that, it's back to the grindstone for me."

"But won't you miss Alex terribly?"

Kathy pulled a wry face. "I'll fly back on days off and sometimes he'll join me in town. It won't be easy but we'll make it work." She dumped her backpack on a chair, looking at the kitchen chaos with interest. "What does a girl have to do to get a cup of coffee around here? I worked up a thirst on the flight into town."

"If you'd let me know when to expect you I would have had the kettle on the boil. I've been baking chocolate brownies so you've timed your arrival well. Take a seat while I finish cleaning up and then we can relax."

"Mm—your cooking was worth coming back into town for." Kathy sniffed the chocolatey aroma appreciatively. "How's Chris? What have you been up to? Any juicy gossip in town?"

"Chris is fine, glad to be home again and recovering nicely. He was around here earlier and was his usual annoying self, so he must be getting better." She took a couple of mugs from the cupboard and set them ready on the benchtop, waiting for the coffee to percolate. "Life has been mundane really and nothing worth reporting and as for gossip? What makes you think I would listen to idle chatter? I've got better things to do with my time."

"As if." Kathy gave a snort. "This town thrives on gossip. It makes the world go round—well, Alice at least. Nobody come into an unexplained fortune, unlikely pairings happened, people left town in a hurry? There must be something entertaining."

Sarah filled the mugs from the pot and handed one to Kathy.

"The best news I've got is that a new stylist has arrived at *Hair About Alice*. I look forward to someone who can do something with this uncontrollable mop of mine. It absolutely has a mind of its own."

"Sarah, I adore your hair, and it's part of what makes you, you. Promise you won't chop it all off."

"We'll see. I'm open to suggestions—something that allows the sophisticated and elegant me to shine through." She drew herself up, and struck a pose that was supposed to portray the well-groomed and chic woman she yearned to be. The effect was marred Kathy half laughing, half choking on her brownie, spraying crumbs everywhere.

"Okay—I look forward to the transformation. Nothing too drastic though." Kathy changed tack. "You haven't updated me on Joel. Seen him lately?"

"There's nothing much to update. He came around to dinner not long after the barbecue but he's been busy since then. He had some pressing business interstate. I get the feeling this association is probably going to stay a friendship, and that's fine by me. No, honestly," she added in response to Kathy's doubtfully raised eyebrow, "we both have busy lives and he has to focus on his new job. It will take him a while coming to grips with that. I'm not expecting anything to come out of it."

Kathy's frown said it all. "Hmm—I was. I expected lots of wonderful things for you." Her tone changed to one of puzzlement. "Actually, I saw him today. He was at the airport. It looked as though he'd just got off a passenger jet, and he wasn't alone."

An icy hand gripped Sarah's insides, but she tried not to show it. Who had been with him? The woman from the photo? She looked enquiringly at Kathy.

"He had a young boy with him. They must have got off the flight together. I didn't know he had any kids."

"No, I don't think he does, but I'm starting to think there's a lot I don't know. Still, it's reasonable given he had a life before he came to Alice. I just don't understand why he's so secretive about it. It makes me wonder what he has to hide and my imagination goes into overdrive." She held up the coffee pot, eyebrows raised. "More coffee?"

The conversation moved onto safer areas, and of course an update on her Flamenco classes.

"I had no idea the classes were on offer," commented Kathy. "I can't wait to see a demonstration."

"Don't hold your breath. I'm not ready to put on a public performance. Watch this space, and even then only if Tomás is my partner."

"Tomás! I don't know how to keep up with you!" Kathy feigned surprise. Sarah smiled. Keep people wondering. That suited her fine.

For once, Sarah was glad it was Monday. At work, over morning tea, she told the office staff about her flamenco class and how much fun it had been.

"Show us, Sarah. Give us a twirl. We'll clap the beat for you."

"I'm hardly an expert. I've only been to one class. The tutors have been dancing for years. Maria started dancing as a child. You can hardly expect me to dance like they do."

They weren't to be put off, and started clapping in a quick rhythmic staccato. "Dance, Sarah—dance!"

She struck a pose, lifted her chin, and with the best stamp her cork sandals could muster, twirled a non-existent skirt and demonstrated the basic steps. They shrieked with laughter.

"You need a proper skirt," Janet, the accountant said. "Something that swishes nicely."

She was right. A pencil skirt or a pair of jeans didn't cut it.

At lunch time, Sarah slipped out and went shopping. She didn't expect to find a flamenco outfit, but she did want a full skirt that could, as Janet had said, swish nicely.

It was harder than she'd thought, especially in the brief time slot she had. A brain wave took her into the local op shop, and after a frantic rifle through the racks of clothes, she found a brightly-coloured skirt that even had ruffles. It was a respectable length, and even better, she had a blouse in her wardrobe that would go with it perfectly. She paid for it and hurried back to work, happy she had something appropriate to wear.

Sarah didn't hover outside the venue that evening. She was there early, keen to make the most of every moment. The same crowd attended, and this week they were more relaxed, as evidenced by the laughter and chatter before the class started.

Sarah hadn't been the only one who had thought about clothing. One woman had gone the whole nine yards and turned up in a red and black dress, similar to the one worn by Maria. Sarah was surprised she didn't also have flowers in her hair. She admired the woman's chutzpah though.

"Welcome, welcome," Tomás called as he swept into the room. "Eet is so good to see you wonderful dancers in back my class." He clapped his hands. "Watch carefully. Tonight we learn ze new steps."

His beaming smile took in the class. Sarah thought it lingered briefly on her, but she couldn't be sure.

The guitarist strummed his opening chords and various feet started to tap. Tomás swept Maria into his arms and the session began. The steps were demonstrated, once, twice, and then the class was instructed to follow. Sarah's heartbeat increased. She turned to her first partner for the evening and throwing out her chest, struck her pose.

The time passed quickly, leaving Sarah flushed and invigorated. There was no escaping the benefits of physical activity on the psyche. If she'd been wearing red shoes, she could happily have kept on dancing.

With Tomás' practice of swapping partners, she now knew a few more people and members of the class lingered briefly before meandering towards the door, still chatting. In keeping with the previous week, Tomás stationed himself at the door, exchanging words of farewell with students.

Sarah hung back, hoping it wasn't too obvious. The lingering farewell from the week before was foremost in her mind, and she wondered about asking if he'd like to join her and perhaps some of the others for coffee. He was handsome, and oh so charming. That level of attention was attractive, though he didn't make her heart flutter like Joel had. Tomás wore his heart on his sleeve, or that was the impression he gave.

If she was making a new start in life, surely that could mean dating too? *Dave told me I should live life to the fullest.* Could she really ask him to join her, or was she making a fool of herself? It was a dilemma. She didn't want to make the next week's class awkward.

As before, he took her hand and held it. "Ah, Senorita; you make ze beautiful dance. You 'ave I t'ink ze natural rhythm. Eet is a pleasure to 'ave you in my class."

Okay. He was just flirting. As far as Sarah was concerned, she had the natural rhythm of a left-footed hippo, but it was nice of him to say it anyway. She quickly forgot the coffee idea. For now, the flirting was nice. More please. She smiled into his eyes, feeling as she did that in her new swishy skirt, she was the epitome of a stunning and talented flamenco dancer. She intended to relish that feeling as long as it lasted.

"Sarah!"

She looked around. Who was that? Where had the voice come from?

A figure was leaning against a tree, partially obscured by the shadows. Her eyes strained against the darkness. "Hello?"

Tomás kept hold of her hand, looking also in the direction of the voice.

"Senorita, you are okay? You want me to stay wiz you?"

The figure detached itself from the tree and moved into the light. *Joel.* In the dim light, he looked brooding and menacing, momentarily startling her. This was not the Joel she knew. What was he doing here?

"It's okay Tomás—I know who it is. I'll be fine—thank you."

He raised her hand and brushed it with his lips, before relinquishing it. "Stay safe, senorita. See you next week."

Sarah smiled at him before turning and walking towards Joel, who waited a few metres away, arms folded. "Joel—what are you doing here? How did you know where to find me?"

"That was a touching scene with Romeo. Am I interrupting anything?"

She experienced a surge of irritation. He'd tracked her down to ask her that? "Don't be silly. Tomás is my tutor. You haven't answered my question."

He didn't respond straight away but looked at her appraisingly. "Mark told me earlier today you were taking flamenco classes. I thought I'd surprise you. Nice skirt."

There was no faulting the grapevine. Chris would have told Mark, and Mark in turn had told Joel. Now they were under the lamplight, the initial perception of moody and ominous disappeared. The man in front of her looked tired perhaps, but still with the charisma that had first drawn her attention. He also looked pleased to see her. That was encouraging.

"You've certainly done that. I heard you were back. Did you have a successful trip?"

He looked away momentarily before looking at her again. "It was eventful," he said at last. "There was no fixed agenda but a few things that needed sorting on the family front."

Those secrets again. Was he hiding something, or did he not trust her?

"Hey, that's fine—I wasn't meaning to pry into your personal affairs." She half expected someone to jump out from behind the door crying "Liar! Liar! Pants on Fire!" Of course, she was curious. Good manners dictated she shouldn't stick her nose in.

"You're not prying, Sarah. It's not something I can talk about." Abruptly, he changed topic.

He gave her a slow mile, the sort that started at one corner of his mouth, and crept upwards towards his eyes, emitting a tide of warmth with it. "I thought of you while I was away. I missed you. I kept thinking of those stars you can see in the Territory, and the stories they tell. I remembered one particular story that's waiting for a happy ending."

"Like I said," she whispered with a catch in her throat, "they're the same stars you see in the big city."

"Except you don't see them, do you? At least, not with the same intensity. There's not the same magic." He tilted his head to one side with a look that was wistful. "I wanted to see you again while I had a moment."

"Only a moment? You could have rung me for that."

"I could have," he agreed, "but that's not the same as seeing you. I don't have much time tonight, but thought I could briefly catch you after your class. That's why I'm here."

As she looked up at him, he grasped her by the shoulders, and dropped a light kiss on her mouth. "I couldn't do that over the phone."

A zillion thoughts chased each other through her mind. She'd mentally decided that theirs was a relationship that was going nowhere. He had no right to stir things up, just when she thought her life was getting back on track.

He was close enough that she could smell the scent she now identified as his. That, and the proximity of his body evoked a reaction she hadn't been expecting. The tingling in her breasts spoke of her own arousal. He looked at her with intensity, a hunger even. It mirrored a need in herself. Wrapping her arms around him, she lifted her face to his.

"Kiss me again," she whispered. "Before you disappear, kiss me again."

Chapter 11

SARAH SURVEYED THE contents of her fridge. Just as well that supermarkets were open on Sundays in Alice. There wasn't much worth eating and certainly not enough for lunches and dinner through the week. Tedious though it was, she needed to re-stock.

Pulling on jeans and a t-shirt, she dragged a comb through her hair and headed out. She didn't need to make a huge effort for shopping.

For once, she had a trolley with wheels that were perfectly aligned. Trawling the supermarket aisles was not her idea of fun. Get in there, grab what she needed, and then get out again. Quickly. That was the plan.

Eggs… yoghurt… orange juice… Joel… *What the?* She froze as she took in the figure up ahead. She hadn't seen him since their last kiss. Just remembering it resulted in a delightful titillating sensation. Who knew a kiss could evoke such feelings?

He'd told her then he would be tied up for a while. He also said he would explain when he could, but had some unavoidable commitments. This was confusing. She'd never met a man before who ran alternately hot and cold.

Joel pushed his own trolley and alongside him was a young boy. Was that the boy in the photo? Without really understanding the reason why, she ducked behind a display that would hide her from view if he turned around.

He didn't. He and his young companion meandered along a couple of other aisles, dumping an odd assortment of things in their trolley and then headed for the checkout. Sarah kept an eye on them the whole time. She had a moment's panic when Joel left the boy and trolley in the line and dashed back to grab a last-minute item, but she quickly pulled back out of view and hovered, hoping she didn't look as guilty and suspicious as she felt. She couldn't say why but she knew she didn't want to speak to Joel at this time. She wasn't dressed for it anyway.

When the coast was clear, she finished her own shopping and headed for home. She was safe there, and could indulge the luxury of examining her feelings. Hopefully no one saw her lurking behind the shelves. That would be something else for people to gossip about.

She didn't have much shopping, but one of life's more tedious tasks was unpacking and putting it all away. She carefully washed the fruit and vegetables first, then re-organised the fridge in general. She had almost finished this chore, when the phone rang.

"Sarah? It's Joel."

"Hi." *What did he want?* She waited for him to speak.

"I thought I saw your car in supermarket car park but couldn't see you anywhere. How've you been?" He sounded awkward. Perhaps this was a universal Sunday morning affliction. If so, she had a major dose.

"Oh well, fine—you know. Not much has changed since I saw you last. How was your week?" she asked. She forced a casual note into her voice. Cool, calm and collected, she told herself. That's me. The ticking of the clock on the kitchen wall sounded abnormally loud as she waited for his answer, the second stretching into forever.

"You're twirling your hair, aren't you?"

"What?"

"You're twirling around your fingers one of those cute little corkscrew curls that bounce around your face."

She let go of the strand immediately. "How did you know?"

"I've watched you. Whenever you're feeling unsure of a situation or in any way uncertain, you start twirling. It's one of those endearing features I like about you."

"*One* of them, huh? What are the others?"

"Now you're fishing. I'll tell you when the time's right." He paused. "I did have a reason for calling you actually."

"More than telling me I'm a hair twirler?"

"For a change, I'm the one extending an invitation. Would you like to join me for a barbecue this evening? I bought a small grill earlier today and it needs christening, once I've got it out of the box and finished putting it together. I hope you'll say yes because I also bought some prawns and chicken shasliks to cook."

"Well… I wouldn't dream of standing between an Aussie bloke and his barbecue. That sounds like a culinary delight and is probably the best offer I'm going to get today." There was a blinked pause. "Oh no, that sounded so rude. I didn't mean for it to come out like that."

"It's okay. I wasn't offended. I'll take that as being a yes. Why don't you get here at six? That will give me time to put the unit together, check it works and get myself organised." He gave a half-laugh. "I'm not quite the natural cook you seem to be, so my repertoire on the basic side. If I can grill it, fry it or burn it, I'm fine. We'll have time for a drink before we eat."

She laughed. "We've all got to start somewhere. I'll bring a salad—that just involves chopping and mixing. I'll teach you some time."

"Sounds good. Can you make enough for three? I have a young guest as well. You'll meet him when you arrive."

"I… sure... There'll be enough for everyone. I'll see you this evening. Look forward to it."

Replacing the handset, she reviewed the conversation. Joel hadn't provided any detail about the boy. Officially, she didn't know anything about him and unofficially she didn't know much either, just that he'd been seen with Joel. Was he Joel's son and if so, where was his mother? What else hadn't he told her? So many questions and so few answers. At least she would have a clearer idea after tonight. It was only then that she realised that she was twirling a tendril of hair.

She didn't often visit the cemetery, but she had to go past it on the way to Joel's apartment, and on impulse left home early with a bunch of flowers and greenery that she had picked from the garden. It was an unorthodox bunch, comprised what was in bloom and what she was able to find, but she knew Dave would appreciate it. He was never one to stand on ceremony.

A few other people were there as well, tending to graves, or cleaning up the leaves and dead flowers. That was only to be expected on a Sunday afternoon. There wasn't much interaction as people tended to be introspective and withdrawn when visiting those who had gone before. Communing with the living was best done elsewhere.

Dave's plot was in a quiet corner for which Sarah was glad. She sometimes sought the solitude when she wanted to think or wanted to feel close to Dave. After that dreadful day of Dave's funeral, she had thought she would never come near the place again, but unexpectedly it had become a place of solace.

Shunning formality, Dave's family and friends had built up the surrounds of the grave with artefacts from the land that he'd known and loved so much. The big stone had become the talking stone, where people sat when they wanted to continue their conversations with Dave Bishop. Sarah made herself comfortable, with the warmth from the stone heating her bottom.

She filled the jar she had brought with her with water from the rainwater tank attached to a central shelter and stuffed the stems of her green offerings into the jar.

"Dave, my love— you probably didn't expect me again so soon. You know I think of you often. I miss you so much and still haven't forgiven you for the way you left me. It was so unfair." A small skink which was sunning itself on the surface of the stone jumped off and darted into the security of the space underneath.

"I wanted to tell you that I'm sort of interested in someone. I know you always said I should find somebody when the time was right but to be honest it was the last thing on my mind. I haven't been ready to 'move on' as a few well-meaning people have told me I should. I'm not sure that I am now either, but there is a man who is new to town and I've been seeing a bit of him lately."

She twisted a strand of hair around her fingers, pondering her next words. "I don't know where it's going, or if it's going anywhere at all but—I just wanted to tell you." She stood up and stretched, her knees giving ominous creaks. "You know I'll never forget you don't you? Never."

~

She could hear voices before she knocked on the door. One voice was Joel's and the other clearly that of a boy whose voice hadn't broken.

She knocked. Footsteps approached before the door was flung open. The boy stood there, looking at her. No greeting, no comment—just staring. Irritating child. She raised a questioning eyebrow. The gesture was wasted.

"Sam? What are you doing? Say hello to Sarah and invite her in." Joel's disembodied voice came from the direction of the kitchen.

"Hello Sam; I'm Sarah. May I come in?"

The boy stood to one side, holding the door open. He didn't say anything. *Hmm. Problem child? One without manners, that's for sure.*

Joel came forward, wiping his hands on a small towel. He took the salad bowl from her, planting a welcoming kiss on her lips. "Glad you could come. This is Sam. He's staying with me over the school holidays."

The scowl on the boy's face indicated he was not altogether happy with this arrangement. He had a shock of unruly hair, almost as dark as Joel's, and eyes of the same colour. It was not hard to see they were related. His mouth was sullen, seemingly in a perpetual pout. He looked to be about twelve, still with some little boy roundness. That would probably disappear with the onset of adolescence. There was no explanation provided on their relationship, which Sarah found odd.

"That should be nice for you both," she said in a neutral tone. "I hope I'm not late. I dropped in on a friend on the way here. Anything I can do to help?"

"I think we're under control. Sam and I mastered the assembly instructions for the grill, and the prawns and shasliks are in the marinade, ready to go on the hot plate. I've got a couple of snags as well, as Sam's not big on prawns. All the more for me, I say." He gestured towards the kitchen bench. "Potatoes are sliced, ready to go and the garlic bread is in the oven. I think that's everything."

He opened the fridge door and took out a bottle of wine. "We can sit down and have a drink and you can fill me in on what's been happening in your life."

He poured a glass of white wine for Sarah and himself, and a soft drink for Sam and then lead them to the courtyard at the rear of the apartment. Here, an outdoor setting was located close to the new barbecue, with the empty packaging still in the corner.

"We've tried it out and worked out which knob does which things. We're reasonably confident we know how to drive it now, and Sam's going to help with the cooking."

"That's great." Sarah hoped she masked her lack of enthusiasm. The thought of overcooked or burnt prawns was not enticing, nor the prospect of undercooked chicken. Should she offer to supervise? Looking at Sam over the rim of her glass, she decided she should butt out on this one. She could always just eat garlic bread and salad.

"So, Sam—how long are you staying in Alice?"

"I don't know. It's only s'posed to be for a little while. I want to go home."

"Now Sam," Joel interjected, "you know that's not possible at the moment. Anyway, you've only just arrived. You haven't seen anything of the town yet."

"What's there to see? It's all boring."

Sarah threw a quick look of query in Joel's direction. His eyes met hers briefly but he just gave a small shrug, as though to say 'Kids!' She wanted to ask about nature of their relationship, but hesitated. Surely Joel would volunteer that information?

"There hasn't been enough time for it to be boring, mate. We might go camping for a couple of days, and then there are the local water holes to explore. We could even go to the drive-in one evening. I don't think you've ever been to one before so now's your chance. You'll have to look in the paper and see if there are any suitable movies showing. There should be, seeing as it's holiday time."

The boy shrugged his shoulders and showed little emotion. He didn't even look at Joel.

"Sounds like this is your first time in Alice, Sam." Sarah stepped attempting to rescue Joel. "Are you interested in planes? I work with an aircraft company so I can take you out to the hangar one day, and we can check out the planes that are in for servicing. If I clear it with the boss, you might even be able to do a short flight on one of the mail runs out to the stations."

"Do you mean fly in a plane?"

She had his attention now. "Yes. Not a passenger jet like you would have travelled in to Alice, but a small aircraft—probably an eight or six seater. The pilot will be delivering mail and other supplies to the stations along the route. Sometimes passengers go along as well. If there's a day when no one has booked seats, you might be able to go along for the ride. You'd have to do exactly what the pilot said of course, and keep out of the way while loading and refuelling was going on. It would give you a chance to visit a few cattle stations."

"Cool." For the first time, he responded positively. "I've never been in a small plane. Coming up here was the first time that I'd been in a big plane and that was really good but I couldn't see much."

"This would be quite different—if it's okay with Joel, of course."

Joel topped up their drinks and lightly biffed Sam on his arm. "We can talk about that. Ready to fire up the barbie, mate? You can show us your culinary skills. You get it going while I bring the food out from the kitchen."

Sam didn't appear overly eager. He swung his feet backwards and forwards under his chair a couple of times, his lips pursed before getting up. Sarah was surprised when he expertly lit the burners. Not totally without skills then. Joel not only brought out the food to be cooked, but an apron declaring the wearer to be *World's Greatest Cook*, which he slipped over Sam's head.

"All good cooks have one of these when they're grilling on a barbecue."

"Yeah—Miguel has one that's got a macho man on the front. It looks like he's just wearing his jocks."

Interesting. That man again and obviously Sam knows him as well. I wonder what the connection is? Perhaps ex-wife's new lover?

"While you two demonstrate your manly prowess with the barbecue tongs, I'll set the table. I assume I'll find what I need in the kitchen?" Sarah asked.

Joel waved the tongs in response. "It's all in there somewhere. Go for it. I think we'll eat out here."

It was a mild evening, and while they had been talking, the sky had morphed through the various hues that heralded twilight and the evening beyond. The temperature had settled to just right—no longer sporting the heat of the day, but Sarah didn't need to put on extra clothing. It was time to just chill and put aside the things that had been niggling at her. Just focus on the moment and the worries might never happen.

She set the table and sat back in her chair to watch Joel and Sam cook, enjoying the chance to relax. Joel evidently knew enough about getting the hotplate to the right temperature before putting the meat on and had everything nicely basted. He'd directed the boy without being over-bearing. The prawns, chicken and sausages all came off the heat at just the right time, still succulent but appropriately cooked.

"Okay—I think we're in business. Dinner is served." With a flourish, Joel placed the platter of hot food on the table. "Help yourself."

They sat down at the table, enveloped by the appetising smell of sizzling meat. Sarah served herself from the platter, and the salad bowl as well. She nodded appreciation to the boy. "Sam, I think you've done well. This the best barbecue I've had in a while."

His mouth full, the boy didn't verbally respond, but she took the head-nod as appropriate acknowledgement. Sam even agreed to eat a little salad, clearly preferring his sausages and tomato sauce.

Discussion returned to entertainment options while Sam was staying with Joel. Joel had some flexibility but activities had to be worked around his schedule as well.

"I'll follow up on the mail run flight," Sarah said, "but it will take me a couple of days to organise, assuming the boss doesn't object of course. I'll get back to you on that."

"All I can offer is a radio station," mused Joel, "and that's not terribly interesting."

The boy perked up. "Yes, it is. Can't I come out with you one day? I want to see how it all works. I want to see all the equipment and technology and stuff."

"I'd like to see it too, and to an outsider it *would* be interesting. You're so blasé about it you forget how radio appears to the person in the street. All I know is that I turn on the radio and a voice or music miraculously appears." She reached for the tomato sauce, delivering a sizable blob to the side of her plate. "Sure, Marconi had a lot to do with the 'how' but beyond that I remain remarkably ignorant about broadcasting. Can I come too—if I'm not being too pushy?" She simpered at Joel across the table, causing Sam to roll his eyes, and then again when Joel reached over and took one of Sarah's hands in his.

"You'd be welcome. Late Monday afternoon would be a good time. We'll be recording the program for younger folks around Alice, *On my Wavelength,* and that might be interesting for Sam."

Sam looked up, a half-eaten sausage speared on his fork. "What's the program about?"

"Listeners can ring in to request their favourite tracks and the interviews are geared towards their interests as well. We try to have of something for everyone at the station but obviously not all at the same time."

"So, I can put in a word to the producers about my choice of music and patter for the program first thing in the morning?" Sarah asked.

He laughed. "Sure—why not? The session starts at four. It would be great if you could pick Sam up as well. Are you able to leave work that early?" He looked at her inquiringly. "He'll be at the swimming pool with the vacation training program. He's already a star performer in the water and he's putting in some extra time."

"I can do that if you're out of the water and ready to go by about a quarter to four, Sam. You need to be waiting out the front so I can just pick you up and go."

"Make sure you don't keep Sarah waiting, mate."

"Nah, I won't." He gave an unexpected grin. "I wouldn't be late for that. Can I go and watch TV now?"

"OK—for thirty minutes and then you need to be in bed. You know the programs you're allowed to watch. Take your plate inside."

"Miguel lets me stay up later than that!"

"I don't care what Miguel does. He probably operates on Spanish time. When you're staying with me, you're going to bed at a reasonable hour."

"S'not fair," grumbled Sam, but he quickly cleared the table and took all the dishes and used utensils inside.

"I'll be in later to tuck you in," Joel called after him. "Don't forget to clean your teeth and say good night to Sarah."

"G'night Sarah." He clearly still was not happy about the bedtime.

"Good night Sam," she called. "I'm looking forward to Monday."

There was no reply. She didn't really expect one.

"You're obviously no stranger to kid-wrangling." It was a not-so-subtle invitation to tell her more.

"You could say that. I've had some experience—with this young man anyway."

If he didn't volunteer any details, she would have to ask. She couldn't organise a work flight for Sam without having some information about him. "I'll need some basic information to organise a flight. Who is he, Joel? What's your connection to Sam?"

Joel shifted uncomfortably and topped up her wine glass. Sarah thought he was buying time. *He's not going to tell me. He's hiding something.*

The silence stretched before he spoke.

"Sarah, Sam is my nephew. It's a complicated situation, but I can't talk about it at the moment. I don't want him to overhear the conversation either."

The stilted words made her feel embarrassed for asking. Sarah covered her discomfort by shrugging and breaking eye contact. She took a sip of her wine. "We all have our secrets, I suppose." She tried to retrieve the situation with some grace.

"He's had some house-training," she commented. "Not too happy to be here though, is he?"

"You noticed? Not very hard, really. It's been a full-on couple of days and I just hadn't realised how draining it could be being responsible for the care and happiness of one unhappy kid."

"So you just asked me 'round for sympathy, did you?" Sarah stood, grabbed his hand, and hauled him up into a tight embrace. He nuzzled into her hair with a small sigh.

"And here was I thinking you wanted to be sociable and to feed me," she murmured into his shoulder.

"Well, that too but right now…" His voice trailed off. "Mm, you smell nice. If circumstances were different, I could show you what being sociable really means. My style is cramped this evening." With his hands on her lower back he drew her closer and pressed her tightly to him. In spite of circumstantial restrictions, he still managed to caress her breast, an action that caused a delicious tingling sensation. It gave rise to conflicted thoughts. She was yet to be convinced that he wasn't full of empty promises.

"Um—I think you've given me a fair idea." At that close proximity, the strength of his ardour was quite apparent. "However, I think not tonight, Josephine. How long is Sam staying?" she asked against his shoulder.

"Not sure. There are a few dramas happening back home so it's best that Sam stays with me for a while. A week or so… perhaps more." He moaned softly, pulling her more tightly into him. "I hadn't planned on a young chaperone. We'll work around it somehow. Kiss me, and then we'll go inside for coffee."

It was a lingering kiss, full of promise and regret. As Sarah told herself when driving home some time later, it was not a relationship that was going to be rushed. It would have to evolve the old-fashioned way, no matter what their intentions. But why couldn't Joel tell her more about Sam? Very strange.

Chapter 12

SARAH ARRIVED AT work an hour early on the Monday so she could leave at an appropriate time to pick up Sam. Even then, she would have to make up some time later in the week. She had some flexibility in her job. Provided she met major deadlines and commitments, there was give and take in how her hours were structured and she took care not to abuse that arrangement.

Cruising towards the swimming pool entrance, she spotted Sam waiting outside. She tooted the horn and slowed down, waving out the window to attract his attention. She pulled over into a no-parking zone and Sam jumped in quickly, allowing her to drive away before upsetting anyone.

"Don't forget your seatbelt. How was your swim? What did you have to do today?"

"Oh, you know—laps and things."

"Do you train with a squad back in Melbourne?"

"Yep."

OK. Back to monosyllables. "Should be interesting at the radio station. I've always wondered what it would be like behind the scenes. Lucky Joel can pull strings for us."

"Yep."

They lapsed into silence for the rest of the journey. The station was on the edge of town, the site marked from afar by the huge telecommunications tower behind it. On entering the reception area, they could hear the current broadcast over wall-mounted speakers. The receptionist looked up in query.

"Help you?"

"We're here to see Joel Pemberton."

"Is he expecting you?"

"Yes, he is. I'm Sarah Hartford."

"Take a seat and I'll let him know you're here." With one perfectly manicured hand, the woman dialled some numbers on her phone and then purred into it, with an entirely different voice. "Joel—there are people in reception to see you. Sarah Harper, I think she said."

"Hartford. My name is Hartford."

The woman flicked her hand dismissively as she hung up. "He'll be here shortly." She turned her attention back to papers on her desk, until the inner door opened and Joel came through. Then she noticeably straightened in her chair and directed a hundred-watt smile in his direction.

A sudden chill gripped Sarah. *So that's the lie of the land.* She felt very dowdy and gauche in comparison with the woman behind the desk. She wore the company uniform to work, and only minimal make-up. At least it was practical. Judging by her appearance, this woman focussed on glamour. Sarah's hackles rose. *Hands off, sweetie—he's mine.*

"Sarah, Sam—you're right on time. I'll get you to sign the visitor log and then you can come through. Thank you, Sophie." Joel threw a quick smile in the receptionist's direction before dropping a light kiss on Sarah's cheek and a proprietary hand on Sam's shoulder.

Smiling in response, Sarah was interested to see Joel in his own environment. He exuded an air of confidence and assurance, which in itself was appealing. It wasn't that he'd portrayed himself as anything but competent before, but now she looked at him in a new light. This was the man, who Sophie saw every day. Today, his attention was directed at her and Sam.

They both signed the log. Sarah made a point of not looking at Sophie again. She hoped the woman noticed that Joel placed a hand in the small of her back as he opened the door and ushered them into the inner sanctum.

The studio from which the current presenter was broadcasting had internal windows of thick glass, so anyone standing in the passage could see inside and observe the action. The red light illuminated above the door indicated the studio was live and no unauthorised entry was permitted. The presenter wore huge earphones, and sat in front of a microphone and a bank of dials and switches. He saw them watching and gave a wave, not pausing his patter.

A woman sat at a desk outside the studio, and Joel explained that she was the program producer. She researched material and topics for the program and helped to coordinate everything. She also vetted incoming phone calls before connecting them to the announcer. Sam's eyes were wide as he took it all in.

"Come this way," said Joel, "and I'll introduce you to Mac. He's the one who presents the *On Your Wavelength* program. He's working on the session's programming now."

If Sarah anticipated meeting a Scot, she was in for a surprise. Mac was an Indigenous man with a broad Australian accent and a grin from ear to ear.

"G'day. Joel told me you were coming. So, you're going to help me, young fella? You'd better come this way. You can help me finish choosing the music. Heard any good jokes lately?"

They disappeared down the passage, leaving Joel and Sarah standing outside the studio.

"Well, I didn't hear a single squeak of complaint," Sarah remarked.

"He didn't moan to you on the way here, did he?"

"No, far from it. Hardly spoke in fact."

"Yeah—he's like that at the moment. He's a good kid really—things have been tough for him at home. He's entering that awkward age; neither fish nor fowl. The attitude is hiding a lack of confidence."

So what's the drama? Why is he here with you?

Oblivious to her questions, Joel led the way down the passage. "Once he gets to know you better, you won't be able to shut him up. Mac's good though. He'll draw Sam out of himself. He's a natural with kids. That's part of why he's got the job he has. C'mon— I'll show you around, though you've seen most of it already."

He showed her the library, and room where Sam and Mac sat with their heads together, in deep discussion. They didn't interrupt. The Sales Manager's office was next, although he was out visiting clients. Then there was a meeting room, the lunch room and Joel's office.

He swept her inside and shut the door behind him. Seizing her, he pulled her close, nuzzling her hair. "Have I told you how delectable you look today? I'd like to have my wicked way with you but I have a feeling that this isn't the right time or place. Familiar story, isn't it?"

It was and Sarah was starting to wish that it wasn't. Reaching up, she pulled his head down to hers, relishing the slow gentle kiss that she teased from him. She could feel her breath quickening and a warm ache in the pit of her belly. Oh God, she wanted more. This was so not fair. She pushed him away. "Unhand me, you wicked man. You're playing absolute havoc with parts of me that haven't been havoc-ed in a long time."

"I look forward to rectifying that situation sometime very soon," he whispered.

Clipped footsteps were heard coming down the passage to his office and they sprang apart just before hearing a brief rap on the door. Without waiting, it opened and Sophie entered, her look flinging daggers at Sarah before turning her attention to Joel.

"I need your signature on these letters if we're going to catch the evening post."

He took the letters and retreated to his desk to look at them and scribbled his signature on the bottom. Sarah smoothed down her skirt and hoped that her lipstick wasn't smudged. No, that was a lie. She hoped that it was and that Sophie had noticed. She smiled sweetly at Sophie but got a stony-faced response. *Good. She's got the message.*

"Thanks Soph. Good work." He handed the paperwork back and turned to Sarah. "We'd better see what Sam and Mac are up to."

To their surprise, they found the pair had moved into the studio and were sitting at the console. They were preparing for a handover from the outgoing presenter who was in the middle of a wrap. Sam sat in front of a microphone too, with a huge set of earphones on his head. He spotted Joel through the glass wall of the studio, and gave him a huge grin and a thumbs-up.

A popular music track began, and the outgoing presenter got up and Mac slid into his place. They couldn't hear what was being said as the mikes were off but watching through the window it was clear some friendly banter was taking place. The music faded and Mac flicked a switch and delivered his opening spiel.

"We've got a great line up of music and interviews for you this afternoon and to be sure of that I've had some help in choosing today's tracks. Stay the distance and let me know what you think. Thanks to Susie G and Annie, who rang in with their suggestions. Stay tuned, girls; you won't be disappointed. To kick us off we have Sam in the studio. Sam, what have you chosen and what do you like about this track?"

After a brief stutter, Sam launched into the reasons for his choice. Sarah guessed this had been rehearsed with Mac in advance. What a nice man to give Sam that opportunity.

The first track played and the producer outside the studio fielded the evening's calls as listeners rang in with requests or comments. The producer cued Mac and put the first of the calls through to him to have a preliminary chat before going live again. As the music faded, he took the call on air and had a slightly rehearsed chat with his caller. Sarah and Joel could hear through the speaker outside the room.

Mac was experienced at putting people at ease and drawing them out of their shyness. He flicked Sam's microphone back on and asked him to tell one of the jokes they had rehearsed before. Canned laughter filled the studio, and Joel signalled to Mac and Sam that it was time that Sam left. With some reluctance, Sam placed the headphones on the desk and slid off his chair. He gave Mac a high five before making his way out of the studio.

"Joel—did you hear me? Wait 'til I tell the kids at school. They'll be so jealous. Do you record the programs? Can I get a copy?"

"Yes I heard you," Joel said. "You did well. I'll cut a copy for you tomorrow. Give me a minute while I grab my briefcase, and we can be off. I'm done here for today."

Sam still enthused about his experience when Joel rejoined them. "That was so cool. I might work in radio when I'm older. Mac showed me what to do. He knows so much, but it looked really easy, once you knew which switch to flick. Can I come again?"

"I guess that can be arranged. We'll talk about that later. I hope you thanked Mac for letting you sit in on his show?"

"Of course, I did. He said I was a big help."

Joel ushered them back to the reception area. They signed out of the visitor's register, and Sarah resisted the urge to slide her arm through Joel's as they headed for the front door. It wasn't really her style and anyway, she was sure Sophie had the message that Joel was not up for grabs. Sam continued regaling them with details of his experience.

It was a healthy change, to see him so animated instead of the morose child with whom she'd tried to interact so far. Kids were an unknown entity. She didn't even know people with kids of this age. If she did, she would have introduced them. She paused at her car. Sam would travel back with Joel.

"Thanks for the opportunity to look over the station. I wasn't sure what to expect but it was interesting. That control panel would take a while to get your head around. I wouldn't know where to look first."

"It can seem overwhelming," Joel agreed, "but it doesn't take long to find your feet. Radio school helps with that." He opened the rear door of his car and threw his briefcase on the back seat. "Does anyone feel like pizza tonight?" He was looking at Sam, whose eyes lit up.

"Pizza? Cool!"

Joel turned to look at Sarah. "I meant you too, of course. You'll have to join us—my treat. It's my thanks for picking Sam up today and bringing him to the station. I'll need your advice though on the best pizza bar in town."

This is unexpected. I didn't have other plans tonight. Why not?

"I'd love to join you. There aren't many choices but my preference is for Perillo's Pizza. If you follow me, I'll lead you there. We can get a park at the rear of the restaurant."

They headed back into the centre of town in their respective vehicles. As it was the beginning of the week, there wasn't much problem in both getting a park or finding a table. It would be different in a few days' time. The restaurant was one street back from the main road and the front of it was lit up with a string of red, green and white lights, whether reminiscent of Christmas or to add an Italian influence, Sarah wasn't sure.

Teenagers and people who wanted to smoke occupied tables on the footpath. The paving showed evidence of stains from bits of pizza, previously dropped and ground underfoot.

Sarah knew some diners in the restaurant, and as they greeted her, she noted their eyes flicking over Joel and Sam. Nothing was secret in this town. Before long, someone would be sure to bail her up to ask about the tall, dark man she'd been seen about town with. *C'est la vie*. A pity there wasn't more to tell, although two dinner invitations in two days must mean something.

"Can we sit by the window?"

Sam didn't wait for a response, but plonked himself down in a window seat.

"I guess we're sitting by the window," Joel remarked dryly. "At least we can watch the view outside."

They spent a few minutes examining the menu and discussing the merits of the various selections. Sarah was happy with whatever, but for Sam it was a serious undertaking. She sipped appreciatively on the glass of red wine that Joel had ordered before they sat down. It was a fitting end to the day.

"So—more training in the pool tomorrow, Sam?"

"Yeah. Another kid there is at the same level as me—though not as good. We're sort of training buddies. It's better when you've got someone else to train with and compete against. He even said I could go around to his place after swimming some time."

"Did he now?" queried Joel. "Does this kid have a name and do you know where he lives? I can't just let you wander off with strangers."

"Sure he's got a name and I wrote the details down. They're in my bag. I do lots of stuff on my own these days. It's not as if I'm a little kid anymore. I can look after myself." He looked around the restaurant, and his voice reflected his excitement. "Look they've got a Jukebox. Can I have some money? I want to choose some music."

"You've caught the DJ bug have you? This could get expensive." Sam rolled his eyes. Obligingly, Joel forked out some money and Sam withdrew to the machine in the corner, where he poured over the available titles.

Joel watched him for a moment, before commenting quietly to Sarah. "I know he's been morose since he arrived, but he's lived with a few dramas in recent years and it shows in his attitude. He tends to expect the worst to happen because that relates to his experience."

"I'm sorry to hear that. Sam's lucky to have you."

"Yeah, well… I do what I can, though that's not much. Let's talk of something else. So how was your day?" He reached across the table to take her hand, his thumb gently caressing her palm in a touch that was tantalisingly intimate. His eyes, fixed on hers, delivered her a message that sent her heart rate up a notch.

Perhaps this was the time to tell him about Dave. How could she expect Joel not to keep secrets from her, when she hadn't told him about such an important person in her life. She needed to explain before their relationship developed any further. On the other hand, it wasn't a conducive environment. She shelved the idea for another day.

"My day was good. I finished early, had some new experiences, learnt some new things and spent some time with a tall, dark not-so-stranger who seemed to promise all sorts of wonderful things. My question now is 'Can he deliver?'"

"You bet he can." Joel delivered the response in a throaty whisper as he leant across the table towards her, his eyes now fixed on her mouth. At that moment, Sam plopped back into his seat. They sprang apart, but not before Sam had taken in the scene before him.

"It's okay. You can kiss her if you want."

Chapter 13

"C'MON SARAH—you can do it." The mechanic grinned encouragingly. "Why don't you enter?"

"I'm not going to make a fool of myself in front of all of Alice Springs. The whole town will be turning out for the Henley-on-Todd, plus bus-loads of tourists, and don't forget the media. Cheering from the sidelines—that's my strength. And coaching. I'll have you guys running like Olympic champions."

"Oh yeah? And just how do you propose to do that?"

"Instead of a mechanical hare, I'll have a device travelling in front of you carrying a six-pack of cold stubbies. That should do the trick."

"You might be onto something there. Perhaps you should patent the idea. Women around the country would use it when they want to whip their men into shape."

"I'll consider that. In the meantime, I'll organise some company t-shirts for you. I'm serious about the coaching. If you all come down to the riverbed just north of the town causeway tonight, we can set up an obstacle course and I'll time you. Running through sand isn't easy and I'll have to whip you guys into shape."

"Ooh, I love a dominating woman. I'll let the others know. What time to you want us there?"

With arrangements sorted, Sarah ticked off the paperwork for her delivery to the maintenance hangar and headed back into town. The main road took her past the radio station. The car radio was on and the banter between the morning presenter and his guest provided the background to her thoughts. She enjoyed knowing the face behind the voice. It made the broadcast seem more personal, as though the announcer was speaking directly to her.

She met more of the radio team a couple of days earlier, when accompanying Joel and Sam to a team breakfast. It was a low-key occasion but significant to Sarah because it was a social event in Joel's world. It proclaimed them as a couple, however loosely defined. Mac was there of course and a few of the others who worked in different timeslots. Sophie looked totally glamorous—ridiculously so for that time of day. That was what Sarah told herself anyway. The woman was frostily polite although the look that she bestowed upon Joel still packed a degree of heat. He seemed oblivious to the variations in temperature, and was equally inclusive of both women.

"Sophie—you remember Sarah, don't you? She's been my guide about town and has eased me into the local social scene. I would have been lost without her."

"Joel, you know you only had to ask," Sophie said. This was delivered whilst flashing a wide-eyed smile, and slightly angling her back towards Sarah. "I was born and bred in this town, so there's very little I don't know. Any time you want to get to know the heart of the Centre, I'll take you around. It will be worth it, I promise."

"That's very generous of you Sophie. I'll keep it in mind." He turned back to Sarah, raising a bottle of champagne. "Sarah, can I tempt you with a glass of champagne and orange, or do you just want to start the day with just the OJ?"

154

He manoeuvred Sarah and Sam towards the other people clustered in conversation and introduced them before leading them to the buffet table. If he was aware of the nuances in the exchange that had just occurred, he didn't show it. Sarah was very much aware. She hadn't met Sophie before the visit to the station as they moved in different circles but knew of her. Alice was like that.

Sarah thought back over the event. What had been very obvious was Sophie's interest in Joel, and the fact that she regarded Sarah as competition. Did she need to be watching her back? Possibly she did, but the only thing she was really sure of was that she wasn't going to engage in a cat fight. No way would she demean herself in that fashion. Joel was a rational sort of guy anyway. He'd prefer someone who was the same. Wouldn't he?

As she contemplated this question, the track playing on the radio faded to a close and conversation with the guest resumed. Paying more attention, Sarah recognised the guest as the president of the local Rotary Club. They were discussing the Henley-On-Todd Regatta. She'd forgotten about the money-raising aspect of the event. This year, the Royal Flying Doctor Service was the beneficiary of funds raised. The radio station would be broadcasting from its mobile unit, as had been the case in previous years. The two men discussed the form of the entrants in the various events, based on past performance.

Hmph. You ain't seen nuthin' yet. Wait until the StationAir team hits the sand. On an irregular basis, company teams had participated in various events, without any results of note. Sarah knew exactly why that was the case. She hadn't trained them. She told Joel as much in a phone call mid-afternoon. She was coaching the winning team. She had her own top-secret strategies.

~

Without having an actual boat in which to train, the team of mechanics had to improvise. They chose the Mini Yacht event as their best option and submitted an entry application. Being boat-less was not an immediate problem, as the river was also waterless. In fact, if the river *did* have any water, it would be a disaster for the event. Clutching the framework of bottomless boats of varying descriptions, the team members had to run the designated course through the grainy river-bed sand. It was hard going but huge fun for those watching.

The men fashioned together a couple of lengths of electrical conduit, with shorter crossbars at designated intervals. This created a framework incorporating a series of rectangular sections. The team members then each stepped into a rectangle created by the structure and picking up the sides, raised their improvisation to waist level. It wasn't quite the same as the boat they would be racing in, but created a sense of team. It also gave them some idea of the challenges of running within the restrictions imposed by the boat. It was flimsy, but the best solution they'd come up with.

Sarah used a couple of pieces of fallen tree branch to mark off the length of the course and lined the men up at the beginning, stop watch in hand.

"Okay—get ready… one… two… three… GO!"

The team lurched forward and staggered erratically for a few metres before the lead man stumbled and they all collapsed into a hooting heap in the sand. Their 'boat' looked worse for the mishap, with the linkages pushed out of alignment. A voice broke in over the general mayhem.

"Call yourselves a team? You're worse than a crew of drunken sailors. You'll never even get away from the starting line, let alone win a race."

Sarah turned at the derisive comments to be confronted by several of the StationAir flight crew.

"And what are you guys up to?"

"We've come to demonstrate how it's done. Can't have this lot showing us all up, can we?

There was momentary silence before the inevitable indignant eruption from the mechanics.

"Oh yeah? You and whose army? What makes you blokes think you can do any better?"

"Just 'cos you can fly a plane, don't think you can sail a boat—particularly this boat."

"You guys are soft. You just sit in a plane all day. Go and play in your own sandpit and leave this to the experts."

It would have developed into more of a verbal stoush if Sarah hadn't stepped in.

"Enough! This is not such a bad idea. Two teams training against each other is much better than just one stumbling through the sand. This way I get to whip two teams of men into shape instead of just one. That makes my day."

"Now look what you've done," moaned one of the mechanics. "You've brought out the very worst in her."

"I must get me a whip before our next training session," said Sarah gleefully. "Somehow, I think I'm going to need it. In the meantime, this will do." She broke off the leafy end from

a tree branch that was lying on the ground and swished it experimentally. It didn't quite have the threatening impact she would have liked, but still made a satisfying whooshing noise.

The interlopers explained they were going to enter the Head of the River event. They didn't have a boat to practice in, either real or pretend. It was time for more creative innovation. Discarding the ridiculous contraption the mechanics had devised, she made the two teams line up one behind the other in the order they would assume when racing in the real boats on the day. She then made each man, except for the leader, place his hands on the shoulders of the crew member in front of him.

"Now—do not drop your hands from the shoulders of the man in front," she bellowed. "For this to work you'll have to run in step. We'll give it a trial run. Right foot first, up to the marker and back again. Get ready, on your mark… GO!"

There was slight improvement in team performance with repeated attempts, although the running style was somewhat stilted. What they gained in coordination, they lost in speed, in spite of Sarah running alongside them and swishing her whip. She hollered with an incongruous mixture of stern hilarity. "Pick up your feet and run! You lot have the forward mobility of a caravan of garden snails. You have to do better than this. I'll change your rosters and cancel all leave if you don't."

"Enough already, enough," panted one of the men as he threw himself down on the sand. It only took one to break ranks before the others followed suit. Running in that loose surface for half an hour was exhausting.

"Do you whip all your men into shape like that? I'm impressed—I think." Joel sat in the shade of a tree on the riverbank. "I'm not sure whether that was the funniest or the scariest thing I've seen for a while." He had a mock look of horror on his face.

Sarah flopped down beside him. Her heart gave a little jig for joy, in spite of her recent exertion. She'd been so engrossed in her training she'd forgotten she'd told him what she was going to be doing after work and where.

She could smell a hint of his now-familiar aftershave. She rather liked it, but there were more pressing issues on her mind. She turned a beseeching gaze on him.

"Joel, this is top secret, you know. You can't tell anyone about our training strategies. No broadcasts or anything like that. These guys are going to win their heats if it kills them."

"Looks like it might do that long before they even get to the event, but my lips are sealed. I won't breathe a word to anyone. I wish I'd brought my camera though. Some of those photos might have had blackmail possibilities."

"I doubt it. Not in this town. Teams of blokes getting whipped up and down the river by a shrieking harridan is commonplace really."

Joel's raised eyebrows indicated his disbelief. "I just dropped in to see how you were progressing and to let you know I recorded the interview with Rose today. After editing the soundtrack and adding some background clips, we'll be broadcasting it early next week. She was a delight, and gave me some good leads on who else I should approach for further talks in this series. It'll be syndicated around the country. I thought you might like to join me for a coffee to celebrate and to say thank you for helping the concept to come about."

Hmm, she thought. *If you want to thank me, I could think of ways other than buying me a coffee. This will do for the interim.*

"So," he interrupted her thoughts. "Can you join me?"

"Sure. Love to. I think we're about done here."

Sarah told the two teams they were free to go and arranged their next training session. She also gave stern warnings about the improvements she expected next time, all of which were all cheerfully laughed at by the men. She then suggested that in the interests of attaining their peak form, they should abstain from drinking alcohol for the rest of the week. This suggestion did not meet with approval.

"She'll be trying to tell us 'No sex' next," exclaimed one of the men indignantly.

"Oh well," she muttered to no one in particular. "It can't be said I didn't try. I can't help it if I'm saddled with a mob of slow-crawling slugs."
~

The late afternoon crowd filled the café but they found a small table near the window. Sarah could smell the enticing aroma of coffee, heightening her anticipation. The two mugs which Joel had ordered were placed in front of them. Even better, they were accompanied by two slices of chocolate fudge cake. *Mm—so wicked. Just as well I don't obsess about my figure.*

"So, is Sam still with you?" She focussed on her cake, making the question sound more like a conversational throw-away line.

"Sure is. He should be here until the Henley-On-Todd and will probably go home the day after. I haven't booked his ticket yet so I must do that." He appraised her over the rim of his cup. "You know, chocolate smudges really do suit you. They give you that sophisticated look of 'Je ne sais quoi'."

"Sophisticated look of a grubby river rat probably."

She wiped at her face and hoped it was to good effect. She had the feeling that Joel had deliberately changed the topic.

"You under-estimate yourself. You look delectable as always, but allow me. You've missed some." Taking the paper serviette from her, he gently wiped at the corners of her mouth, smiling as he did. "Did anyone ever tell you what kissable lips you've got?

Flushing, she snatched back the serviette. "Next thing you'll be spitting on it before wiping my face. That is one humiliation I could do without, thank you very much."

As a rebuke, it went nowhere. He just smiled that irritating smile and again, changed topic. "I'm looking forward to this Regatta, especially now I've witnessed some of what it entails. I should get some good interviews for the syndicate as well. Did I tell you I'd be manning the radio booth on the day?"

"Not specifically, but I heard on a broadcast earlier that there would be on-site coverage. Don't forget to mention the brilliant wins by the StationAir teams."

"I would be delighted to—provided they win of course. Is there an award for the team that comes last?"

"There probably is—a bucket of sand or something like that. For the sake of our teams, that had better not be the result for them."

He laughed. "You're a hard task-master. With you brandishing the whip, I don't think they would dare. Is that how you bend all men to your will?"

"Not all of them. I have a few other charms, as well you know." She gave him a low-lidded look. "Some just make men fall at my feet."

Joel leaned forward, his eyes fixed on hers. "I can believe it. I'm not going to be able to sleep tonight for wondering what they might be. Perhaps you could show me some time?"

Sarah also leant over the small café table. "Name the time and the place. I'll be there," she delivered in a low husky voice, trailing a finger down his chest.

"Hold that thought, sweetheart. I'll keep you to that promise. Even the thought is going to keep me on tenterhooks."

Sarah held his eye. Before she lost her nerve, she needed to get this out. "Joel, I need to tell you about Dave."

"This sounds serious. I haven't met him, have I?"

"No, and you couldn't have—not unless you were here more than a year ago." She bit her lip before continuing, speaking slowly to avoid a catch in her voice. "Dave was my fiancé. He also worked for StationAir as one of their pilots. That's how we met."

"What happened? Where is he now?"

"He's … well …" She hesitated, struggling with the lump that rose unbidden in her throat. "Chris isn't the only one who ended up in hospital. Dave fell ill with leukaemia. It wasn't a long illness, but it was vicious. He died a little more than two years ago. That's who I visited on the way to your barbecue the other night. He's buried in the town cemetery not far from your apartment."

Joel sat back in his chair and took a breath. He looked shocked. "Sarah, I'm so sorry. I had no idea. I gathered from comments Chris had made that something had happened, but never imagined it was an event like this." He shook his head in commiseration.

"I'll never forget Dave, you understand, but I'm not locked in the past either. When we knew there wasn't much time left, we were able to talk about what that meant for us. He was adamant I should live my life to the fullest, making up for the fact that he couldn't. It sounds trite, I know, and it's been so very hard, but recently I've tried to do that."

She had to look away. The sympathy in his eyes threatened to undo her. She pressed her lips together hard to hold the tears at bay. "I wanted to tell you myself. In a town like this, nothing's secret for long. It hasn't been an easy year, and I would never have survived the dark times if it weren't for the support of good friends. I haven't forgotten him— won't ever forget him—but I'm ready to move on."

He reached across the table and took hold of her hand. "Thank you for telling me. It helps me to understand. Words sound so empty at a time like this, but don't ever feel you have to keep quiet about him. If you want to talk about him, or even just mention him in passing conversation, that's fine with me." He looked intently into her eyes. "Seriously, Sarah. Any time you want to talk, I'll listen. That's been a helluva year for you."

Her eyes welled with prickling tears. Sarah took a deep breath, not wanting to dampen the moment with waterworks. She had to pull her hand away from Joel's so she could grab the scrunched-up paper serviette and blot her eyes.

"Thanks. I don't talk about Dave much, to be honest. I'm not hiding anything, but the memories have been raw, and I've needed time to process my grief." She risked a glance back at Joel. "It would be wrong to say I'm over him. I'll never forget him, but we talked about this before he died. He always said that when I was ready, I should move on with his blessing."

Now her nose began to run, and she had to put the serviette to yet another use. It was embarrassing.

They sat in silence for a while. With his elbow on the table, Joel massaged his chin with thumb and forefinger as he absorbed what he'd learnt.

"Sorry," Sarah said. "I didn't mean to put a dampener on the occasion."

"Don't be silly. I'm glad you told me. I need to make a move though. I have to pick up Sam from the pool." He stood up. "I'll be busy-ish on the day of the Regatta but make sure you come and see me in the tent. Once again, thanks for introducing me to Rose."

Just thanks for that? I hope you see me as more than an introduction agency, especially now I've shared so much with you.

They parted at the entrance to the arcade. Sarah watched as Joel strode up the street, his mobile phone already clutched to his ear. Telling him about Dave had been cathartic. It paved the way for a more open relationship with Joel. Why did she sense he still kept secrets? Did this mean he wasn't ready for a more open relationship with her? Didn't he trust her? Once the thought was in her head, it was hard to repress.

Chapter 14

THE FOLLOWING SATURDAY, the day of the Regatta, was beautifully sunny with no suggestion of rain. Water in the river would ruin everything. Sarah had coached the teams on another two occasions, and although they were never going to break speed records, there had been some improvement. She consoled herself with the knowledge that every competitor would be battling the same difficult conditions. It was after all a fun day to raise funds for the Flying Doctor. She would keep telling herself that and not get too intense when their races were scheduled.

Kathy stayed in town for the weekend. She parked her car at Sarah's, and the two women walked down to event location together. It was only a fifteen-minute stroll from Sarah's flat.

"I heard all about your training program, Sarah. You really pushed those guys. Good on you. That was an opportunity too good to miss."

They both laughed. It was good to share some girl time.

"Have you caught up with Joel lately?" Kathy asked.

"I have. He showed me and Sam over the radio station recently and we had a quick cup of coffee in town mid-week. He told me he had recorded the interview with Rose and that after editing, it should go to air in the next few days. I'll let you know when I have an exact date and time. If you're flying when it's broadcast, I can record it for you."

"Thank you—that would be good. So Sam, he's …?"

"Yes, he's the boy you saw with Joel at the airport and no, I don't know anything much about him, except he's a fairly typical kid for his age, and he's Joel's nephew. Joel didn't tell me anything else. There must be some problems at home, but I don't have any further information."

"At least you know that much. Did you find out who Miguel was?"

"No, only that Sam knows him as well because the name has come up in conversation. They all seem to be quite cosy."

Chris's suggestions about the relationship kept running through her mind, but she wasn't going to embarrass herself by repeating that to Kathy. It was too silly for words, so why couldn't she dismiss it? "It's none of my concern. I'm not even sure about where Joel and I are headed, nor whether we are headed anywhere in particular. Being inquisitive about his past is probably out of order."

"I don't think so. If you're going to get involved with anyone, you need to know what baggage they're bringing with them. That's perfectly reasonable. Don't you think it's time for an open book session? How can you trust someone if it appears they're concealing things from you?"

"You're right, I know. There are questions that just seem to be no-go zones for now. No doubt I'll find out more when the time's right."

They had reached the gate for the event, and paid their entrance fee. Sarah surveyed the crowd. "C'mon, let's find the others and claim a good spot for watching everything. I want some shade and a clear, unobstructed view—a location from which the men will hear me yelling at them."

"Just swing that whip I've been hearing about. As long as they can see that, they'll take off like rockets. It won't matter whether or not they hear you over the crowd."

Sarah hoped Kathy was right.

The fenced off event area was filling quickly. Sarah spotted some Aboriginal kids from one of the surrounding town camps scooping a hole under the fence so they could slide under it. She considered remonstrating with them for all of a couple of seconds. They probably didn't have the entrance money anyway, and who was she to spoil some fun for a few kids? Still, after those urchins had wriggled through, she pushed the sand back into place. No sense in enabling a free-for-all.

The two women kept running into people they knew. It was a prolonged meet and greet session before they established themselves in their chosen vantage point along with a bunch of StationAir staff. The organisers called for the participants in the first event to take their places. Anticipation rose in the crowd, and chatter dropped down a decibel as they turned to view the race track. The teams, each wearing identifying colours lined up with marshals directing them to the starting line. The race caller began his warm-up patter, describing the teams, their sponsors, the colours, and of course their attributes. Cat-calling came from the side-lines and probably a few illegal bets were laid as well.

Finally, the starter took his place, called for silence, readied the teams, waited the length of a dramatic pause and then fired the gun. They were off! There was much hilarity as the teams lurched and staggered through the sand. The lead runner on one boat stumbled and slipped to his knees and his team mates were dragged down with him. They pulled themselves upright but by the time they managed to get moving again, had lost their lead position. The crowd cheered them on with the support that the under-dog usually attracts.

The crew made a valiant attempt to catch up and were nipping at the heels of the next boat by the time the winning line was reached.

The excitement wasn't totally over. There was a dead heat between two of the other boats and a photo was called for to decide the winner. Supporters of each team taunted each other until judges handed down a decision, resulting in the eventual winners celebrating with an impromptu war dance. The drama soon settled. Those teams were cleared from the course, the sand raked over, and the Marshalls organised the competitors for the next event.

The events in which the StationAir crews were entered weren't due to be held for a while, so Sarah wandered up to the radio tent to see what was happening there. Mac sat at the controls, and Joel stood to the rear of the tent, overseeing procedures and selecting people for random interviews. A representative of the Royal Flying Doctor Service was their current on-air guest. Sam stood outside the tent, eyes wide and taking it all in.

"How's it going, Sam?"

"Great. Joel told me we were going to see a boat race, but I never thought it would be like this. It's crazy, but a little bit fun as well."

"Just wait, it will get a lot crazier before the day is over, especially the battle at the end. Then you need to duck for cover. With the water cannons and flour bombs, anything can happen."

Sam seemed to be impressed and she was pleased he had found there were a few interesting things happening in Alice. Perhaps he would enjoy his visit after all. She waved to Joel, letting him know that she was there. He gave her a nod in response, flashing five fingers, indicating he would be out in five minutes.

As soon as the interview was finished, he shook hands with his guest, ushered him out and came to join Sarah and Sam, giving her a quick kiss in greeting. There was a just audible snort from Sam, but the boy didn't say anything.

"Hi Gorgeous," Joel said in greeting. "Fantastic weather you've turned on for us."

"I do my best. Don't forget you have to report on the impressive wins from the StationAir teams."

"If they keep their end up, then I'll keep mine up too. Give me the details of their events so I can watch out for them."

"Joel, are you covering the running of the next event? You'll need to come down with me to the starting point if you are."

To her surprise, Sarah saw Sophie lay a possessive arm on Joel. She hadn't expected the woman to be at the event, much less getting up close and personal.

"Ah, no. Mac is covering this one."

"Okay. Perhaps Sam would like to come down with me then?" Sophie kept her hand on his arm, all the while gazing up at Joel.

"Sure—if he'd like to." Sam nodded enthusiastically. "Sam, stay close to Sophie and don't get lost."

The pair set off, Sam without a backward glance but with Sophie throwing a swift triumphant glance in Sarah's direction, a glance that said 'I'm the one needed here.' Sarah quickly looked away, careful not to make eye contact. *You're not the only one to make yourself useful. Two can play at that game.*

"Well," Sarah said, "how nice that the station employees are taking Sam under their wing. It makes it easier for you when you're here in a working capacity. Tell you what—if Sam is at a loose end after this race starts, he can come down to our pitch later. He might like to watch our events with us. It's sure to be exciting at that time."

"Sounds like a plan to me. I'll put it to him when he and Sophie come back. In the meantime, how about a drink? We've got ice-cold cans to give out as part of the station promo, and for special people, we have a drink cooler and a cap as well."

"For special people? I'm honoured. I'll pass on the cap but a drink and the cooler sounds like a great idea. The day's warming up nicely."

A steady stream of tourists and locals alike came past the booth, and as she was standing there, Sarah helped for a while in handing out the drinks and promotional material. She knew many of the locals, and a few stopped to chat, or to enquire if she had a new job.

"No, the pay's lousy. In fact, there's none. I'm helping out for a while. By the way, have you met Joel... the new station manager?"

She was initially in a quandary as to how to introduce him.

This is my new friend Joel...

This is Joel. He and I are seeing each other now ...

Joel and I, um we're sort of, well... It wasn't so difficult after all. She ignored the whole thing and remained non-committal. She was introducing a newcomer to town. Simple. Chris and Mark came by of course and were happy to claim their free drink.

"Curly—have you jumped ship now? I thought you'd be supporting the crew." Chris claimed his drink with mock indignation. "I've heard all about your training program and now you've abandoned them in their final hour of need."

"And hello to you too. Of course, I haven't abandoned them. I'm just having a change of scenery and helping Joel out for a while. I'll wander back to the group shortly to give them a pep talk and get them focussed on their teamwork and strategy. They wouldn't have a hope without me, but I think I managed to whip them into a winning shape."

Mark made a strange sort of snorting noise and it looked as though soft drink was coming out of his nose.

"Mark, sweetie—are you okay? Do you need someone to thump you on the back?"

Chris chortled with unconstrained glee. "Perhaps you could whip him, Curly. That might do the trick."

"Get lost, the pair of you. Just make sure you're cheering at the right time. I'll know if you don't."

As they disappeared, still chuckling with mirth and making wisecracks to each other, Sophie and Sam made their way back to the tent. They had seen a couple of heats for the first event and Sam gave a report on the strange boats in the races.

"This is the craziest boat race I've ever seen. I saw some guys in camel costumes. They said they were ships of the desert." He giggled as he tried to demonstrate their running style. "They couldn't keep up with a submarine. The Americans from Pine Gap were racing in that one. It was painted with stars and stripes." He described every nuance of what he'd seen and heard.

"With an eye for detail like that," Joel remarked, "you might make a good reporter one day. We'll have to keep an opening for you at the station."

The boy blushed, and Sarah thought it was amazing what a little constructive praise could do.

"Sam, I have to go back to the StationAir people now— the first of our events will be staged soon and I've been coaching the teams for a fabulous win. Do you want to come down and help me cheer them on?"

"Okay—I've got a camera. Should I take some photos for you? You know—showing everyone the winning team?"

"Photo-journalism no less! I'm impressed. You're a fast learner. Sure, that would be good. We'll see you in a while

Joel. Bye Sophie." Sarah delivered this last farewell with a sweet smile. It was not reciprocated.

The crowd had increased by this stage, and groups set themselves up on picnic rugs or folding chairs. Tiered seating provided a better view for those who arrived early enough. Food stalls did a roaring trade, aided by the festive atmosphere. Sarah and Sam had to weave their way around the groups. Mostly the adults sat and chatted, but the kids roamed in excitable packs, eyeing off the stalls. The smell of barbecued sausages and onions was enticing, and the lucky ones with money in their pockets lined up either there or at the soft drink stall.

Some kids wore school-branded t-shirts, and Sarah guessed they would be participating in the school events later in the day. Others wore novelty hats or carried pirate cutlasses and eye-patches or some similar costume indicative of the theme for their particular race. They shrieked and jostled with each other, sliding down the riverbank and kicking up the sand.

Sam regarded them with the apprehension of an outsider and moved closer to Sarah as they made their way through and around the crowd. Her group spread themselves over a series of picnic blankets, and looked up as Sarah called out to signal her return. She introduced Sam to her colleagues and they obligingly re-shuffled their seating arrangements, making room for the boy.

"Get in close, mate," said one of the mechanics. "You'll have a front-row seat here. You have to cheer really hard so we can hear you as we come running down the straight. That'll help us run faster. If it looks like we're not coming first, I want you to slip out quickly and trip the other mob up."

"Jimbo," scolded Sarah, "don't you dare put such ideas into his head. Sam, don't listen to him. He's only joking. He's trying to avoid the bollocking he knows he'll get if he doesn't give a winning performance today."

"Shucks Curly—you're no fun at all."

Sarah rewarded Jimbo with a glare, and moved into coach mode, reminding the team of their agreed strategy and generally pumping them up. The marshals broadcast a request for all participants in the Mini Yacht event to 'move up behind the starting line and to get into position please'.

The crew got a thumbs up or general equivalent from their remaining colleagues and ambled off, no sign of tension or adrenaline, much to Sarah's dismay. *Don't these guys ever take anything seriously?* They grabbed their allocated boat from the storage area and took up their position at the starting line.

The starter's gun fired. The crowd roared with excitement. Boats and crews set off at a cracking pace. Sarah had told the StationAir team to focus on running steadily for the first leg of their event. They had to pay attention to their coordination, hoping to maintain their position while others wore themselves out with too much initial effort. Sarah instructed them to go flat out on the return leg.

The team coming first approached the buoy from the left. The next boat approached it from the right. Crack. Timber met timber, and both crews were cast sideways into the sand. That left StationAir and another two boats in the running.

"Now, StationAir—RUN!" screamed Sarah, jumping up, her hands clenched into fists. Beside her, Sam yelled support, his fists pumping the air. It was close—very close. One boat slipped back, leaving two in a battle for front position. The crowd screamed at fever-pitch. With a last burst of energy, the StationAir boat inched ahead at the last minute and won by a squeak.

Their colleagues erupted into cheers. Squealing with delight, Sarah grabbed one of the pilots next to her in an over-excited bear hug. Sam moved back a pace to a position of safety, a look of consternation on his face.

There was much back-slapping when the winners rejoined them, with pointed digs to the next competing team about the standards they now had to meet. The celebratory mood ramped up a notch, and the StationAir supporters settled down again to watch the next event. Sam offered his congratulations as well, and said that it was a good win but he might go back to re-join Joel.

"Mac's back in the radio tent. I want to watch him working and maybe he can show me some more stuff."

"Okay Sam. Thanks for joining us. Don't forget to cheer for the StationAir team when they run the next event. Probably won't be for another half an hour. Shall I walk back with you?"

"Nah—I know where the tent is. See ya later Sarah." With a wave, he disappeared into the crowd. Sarah watched him for a while, but he was heading in the right direction.

The day heated up—hotter than she expected. She wore a hat, and kept to the shade where possible, but even so the day was warm.

"Hey Curly—do you want a celebratory beer?" Mark offered her a can.

"I don't drink beer. It's not to my taste."

"Sorry! We're right out of Moët. It's nice and cold; you might even get to like it."

She accepted the proffered can and took a tentative swig. It was cold and yeasty, and different to the sweet soft drink she'd had earlier. Mark was right. It was a good choice on such a hot day.

She sat down and joined in the general conversation, listening while Kathy described her attempts to give a hand with mustering.

"I don't think I'm cut out to be a jillaroo. I go in one direction and the cattle go in another. I'm not confident on the bikes yet. Give me a plane any day."

"Give it time. Stay safe on those bikes though. In that sort of country, it's easy to hit a rough patch and come off. I'd hate to see you break a leg, or worse."

"At the speed I travel, it's not such a problem."

Sarah relaxed. It was such a pleasant day. She would wander back to the radio tent later to see how Joel was faring. For now, she was happy to stay with current company. There was a steady supply of beer, and a pile of empties collected to one side, ready to be taken to the bins at the end of the day. Sarah nursed her drink, though the men added to the empties' pile at an impressive rate.

Gradually, the pressure in her bladder became uncomfortable. Only reasonable, given the amount she'd had to drink. If she hurried, she could make a quick trip to the toilets before the next StationAir race.

Bracing herself against Kathy's shoulder for leverage, she stood, wobbling as the blood rushed to her cramped legs. A wave of dizziness sweep over her. Her vision dimmed in the bright sunlight. Clutching her hands to her eyes, she swayed unsteadily.

"Steady on Curly, are you okay?" Jumping up, Chris reached out and grabbed hold of her arm, holding her firm.

"Give me a moment, I'll be fine. Just stood up too quickly that's all."

She took her hands away from her eyes, and blinked cautiously. Everything came back into focus.

As her vision cleared, she saw Joel standing in front of her.

"Where's Sam?"

"What do you mean, 'Where's Sam'?" She squinted at him, feeling bewildered. Why was he asking? "He's with you. He went back half an hour ago."

"But he was supposed to stay with you. He knows not to wander off on his own."

"I doubt he's far away. He wanted to catch up with Mac again so was heading back to the radio tent."

"I haven't seen him. Dammit Sarah, I trusted you with Sam and now you've no idea where he is." His gaze swept over the group, taking in the incriminating empty cans. "I don't have to ask what you've been doing. Falling over inebriated seems to be a habit."

"That's not fair." *He has no right to make insinuations like that. In front of my friends; how dare he?*

"Steady on," interjected Chris. "You're being rather unreasonable. Sam's not a little kid. He'll be around here somewhere. He's found something interesting to watch. He'll turn up soon."

Joel turned a death stare on Chris. "I'm responsible for Sam. If anything happens to him, the consequences don't bear thinking about. You don't understand the implications. He's under strict instructions not to wander off. The last thing I need is a drama surrounding that boy."

His lips compressed into a thin line. He glanced briefly at Sarah, then looked away, avoiding eye contact. He began to walk off, stopped a short distance away, and looked back. His open-handed gesture asked the question that was in his eyes; *how could you?*

"I'll help you look for him," Sarah called, taking a couple of steps towards Joel. *She had to do something to make things right. Why was he behaving like this?*

"Don't bother. You wouldn't get too far in your current state. Stay where someone can look after you." He looked at

Chris, and the inference was clear. Joel strode off, leaving an uncomfortable silence behind him.

"Well fuck him, if that's his approach. He's not going to win friends with an attitude like that," Chris said.

"I should have walked back with Sam to the radio tent," wailed Sarah. "I thought he'd be fine by himself."

"Look, he won't be far," said Kathy. "The area is fenced off and he's unlikely to have wandered out through the gates."

"What if he's been kidnapped though? He could be anywhere." She looked over her shoulder, as though Sam might miraculously re-appear. "I'm going to go and look. I can't stay here doing nothing."

"Okay. I'll come with you." Kathy stood up, brushing the sand from her legs and looked around their immediate vicinity first. "Joel headed back towards his tent, so why don't we look in the other direction?

With a quick trip first to the public toilets, they fought their way through the crowd, scanning faces and any group with children, which meant most of them. It seemed an impossible task, but then Sarah spotted him, chatting with a group of other kids. Breaking away from Kathy, she stormed up to them, grabbing Sam by the arm.

"Sam—what are you doing here? Joel's been worried. He's looked everywhere for you." Her voice was louder than she intended.

The boy was indignant. He flushed and tried to pull his arm away. "I'm okay—I ran into Michael. We do swimming training together."

"You know you have to let Joel know where you are. He's been worried about you. Ask him first before you run off with your mates. C'mon. I'll walk back with you."

"Do I have to? The next race is about to start." The whine bordered on petulance.

"Yes, you do. Joel is responsible for you. He wants to know where you are and who you're with at all times. If we hurry, you'll have plenty of time to see the race."

As they approached the radio tent, they could see Joel at the front, anxiously scanning the crowd. Sophie stood alongside him with a possessive clutch to his arm. Sarah decided she'd come close enough. She grasped the boy's shoulder.

"There's Joel. I'll leave you to it. Good luck. Remember—he's only concerned for you."

She gave the boy a shove. After seeing him move in the right direction, she turned back to where Kathy waited. She looked back over her shoulder and saw Joel had spotted them. He reached out towards her and made as if to speak. She looked away quickly before he could say anything, wishing she could just vanish. She wasn't looking for any further humiliation.

"He's okay now Kathy. We can get back to the others."

"But don't you want to…"

"No, I don't."

Chapter 15

"I DON'T BELIEVE it. How could they do this to me?"

"Do what Curly?"

Even the mechanics had adopted the name.

"Don't call me that. Look at this."

The front page of the Centralian Advocate lay on her desk. It featured a write-up of the Henley-on-Todd, and the photo depicted the StationAir staff, celebrating their win, cans of beer clearly visible. Centre stage was Sarah, jubilant and pumping her fist in the air. Chris was alongside her, one arm loosely draped around her shoulders in triumphant camaraderie.

"That's good, isn't it?" He was clearly puzzled.

"Look at me. I'd hardly had a drink at that stage and already I look out of control and under the weather."

The picture was in full colour and the caption read *Rivers of Cheer*.

"It might as well have said *Rivers of Beer* because that is what it looks like."

The mechanic peered again at the paper, wondering what he was supposed to see.

"It looks to me like a bunch of happy people celebrating a win. I thought that's what you wanted."

"A win, yes but not to look like I can't stand up."

The look he gave her was confused. He opened his mouth as if to say something and then shut it again and left the office shaking his head. Sarah folded the paper and tossed it in the waste bin so she didn't have to look at it any more.

She hadn't noticed the photographer, but at the time, she'd been too excited to see anything other than a great result. Once Joel saw that photo, and of course he would, his opinion of her would be confirmed. She was just a party girl who couldn't handle her drink and couldn't be trusted to look after a child. Well, one particular child.

Sarah was still distraught later that afternoon when she caught up with Kathy. Her friend was staying in the town house. Sarah made a detour after work and dropped in for a consoling chat.

"Cup of tea, or glass of wine?"

"Tea. It has to be tea. I'm never drinking again. It always seems to get me into trouble."

"Don't you think you're over dramatizing?"

"You saw the way Joel looked at me. It made me feel so small. I should have taken better care of Sam. I should have—"

"Now hang on. You *shouldn't* have done anything. You're not the one who brought Sam to the event with an obligation to take care of him. You weren't the one who gave Sam permission to leave the radio tent. Let's keep things is perspective here." Kathy was hands-on-hips indignant. "Joel is the one who was so preoccupied in his work he let his attention stray from *his* responsibilities. I think he's trying to minimise his guilt by transferring it onto you."

"Do you think so?"

"I'm positive."

"You could be right I suppose—but still, I should have made sure he got safely back to Joel."

Kathy sighed. "You're a hopeless case Sarah. Didn't I just say you should've nothing? You haven't listened to a word I've said. If he's the man I thought he was, he'll apologise to you. Just wait and see. If he doesn't, then I wouldn't waste any further time on him."

Sarah wasn't so sure about that but kept her thoughts to herself. It wasn't worth fretting over something highly unlikely to happen.

Besides Kathy, there was only one other person she wanted to talk to; Dave. On the way home, she detoured past the cemetery, pulling up under the shade of a large eucalypt. She picked her way through the graves, seeking solace from the man who lay beneath the big stone. She flopped down on that stone, addressing the person she once thought would always have her back.

"Here I am, back again. Everything's gone pear-shaped, Dave, and he thinks it's all my fault. I thought my life was about to change, but I was so wrong. I don't know who to trust anymore."

She sat for a while, massaging her temple, as though that would dissolve the stress. A light breeze blew up, making the dead leaves dance around her. She brushed the hair from her eyes as she watched their flittering path. They were a welcome distraction, dancing around the graves with a soft whispering sound marking their progress. It didn't matter what direction they followed; each leaf was still at the mercy of the wind. It was a lesson.

"That's me—a small leaf blown this way and that. I need to rely on myself, instead of reacting to the views of others. I thought I'd learned that lesson. Thank you, my love. I'll leave you in peace."

An apology hadn't been offered by the time Chris rang her later in the week. She was in the wind-up phase of the day, trying to think what had been on her to-do list that morning and what she'd actually achieved. Probably quite a lot if she thought about it, but all she really wanted to do was go home, if she could do so without getting wet.

The day after the Henley-On-Todd event, the weather deteriorated and rain had set in. The downpour since then was steady and whereas initially the rain had soaked into the parched earth, gutters and rain tanks were now overflowing and the landscape was taking on a distinctly soggy appearance.

"Hey Curly, what gives?"

"I don't know. Why don't you tell me?"

"Well aside from the fact that miserable weather has grounded me and I'm well and truly over it, I thought you might like to go out for dinner. I've got the all-clear from my aviation medical, and you might like to celebrate with me."

"Dinner? When?"

"Yes dinner, and tonight of course, unless you have a better offer?"

"Well, I'll have to consult my diary. I've already turned down the Crown Prince of Monaco and have a Wall Street stockbroker on hold on the phone. I'm so exhausted with my busy social life I was thinking it might be an ideal night to wash my hair."

He didn't miss a beat. "Great. Why don't I pick you up in my chariot at seven? I'll even pull into the driveway so that you don't have to get wet. This weather's enough to drive anyone stir-crazy. It will do us both good to get out."

"You're probably right. I'll tell the stockbroker to take a raincheck."

"Good. I've got to run. See you this evening, okay?"

Sarah had listened to the radio in the car on the way home. She took note of the warnings about the flooding forecast in the Todd River, and in some of the adjacent low-lying areas. It didn't happen often, but when the river came down, it swept away everything in its path—campers, rubbish, broken branches—the lot. With the riverbed usually dry, some of the local Indigenous people or their visitors often camped there but they knew enough to clear out when the weather was like this. It was fortunate the Regatta hadn't been washed out.

When he pulled into the driveway a couple of hours later, the rain had settled to an intermittent drizzle. Sarah left the outside light on, and made a dash for the passenger side of the car, throwing herself inside. Puddles lined the driveway and in spite of the short distance, she still managed to get mud spatters up the sides of her trousers as she ran. Not a good start to the evening.

"You could have picked a better night," she huffed. "Alternatively, we could have ordered take-away."

Chris flicked his trademark grin, accompanied by a quick pat on her knee. "Where's your spirit of adventure? It's a fabulous night to get out of the house." He carefully reversed out of the driveway. "I thought we might go to Perillo's. They do fabulous cannelloni and on a night like tonight, that would be just the thing."

Her heart sank. That was where she had gone with Joel and Sam. With the memories of that night still fresh, it was the last place she wanted to go. What if Joel was there again?

She couldn't think of a valid reason to go somewhere else, especially as she didn't want to discuss her relationship with Joel. It was only a five-minute drive from her apartment to the restaurant. While she was dithering, Chris pulled up in the car park, with the red and green lights around the restaurant veranda still flashing through the rain. Too late. She would have to wing it.

Inside, the restaurant was cosy and inviting. Best of all, it was dry. The noise enveloped them as the door slammed shut, and the waitress moved forward to greet them and show them to a table. She was the owner's daughter and had worked there for years. Not surprisingly, she knew most people in town.

"Hi Sarah. Good to see you again. Where would you like to sit?"

Sarah had a moment of panic. Please, Maria—don't mention my last visit. She avoided eye contact to discourage further conversation.

"Somewhere quiet please. A table towards the back would be good."

"Don't you want to sit near the window?" queried Chris. "You usually like to see what's going on."

"There's not much to see on a night like tonight. Every time someone opens the door, a blast of wind comes in so sitting further away would be more comfortable."

"Whatever you say, Curly."

She sighed and rolled her eyes. Maria left them with menus and took their order for drinks. Her mood called for a dramatic double whiskey, but she settled for a glass of Shiraz.

A quick glance at the other diners reassured her Joel was not there. She knew she was being paranoid, but she was not ready to run into him again. She couldn't avoid him, in a town the size of Alice, but it would be a long time before her feelings of humiliation faded. Worse was knowing no one was to blame but herself.

Chris fiddled with the cutlery, shuffling knives and forks from one side to the other and then back again. He wasn't normally a fiddler. She wished he'd stop. It was getting on her nerves.

"Sarah, I really wanted to thank you. You were a tremendous support while I was ill—not just getting me to hospital as quickly as you did but visiting me all the time. Doing my washing and keeping everyone up-to-date on my progress was above and beyond the call of duty. You even managed to calm my mother down, and that's saying something."

"You don't have to thank me. I just did what any friend would do, and as for your mother—of course she was worried. I knew she was in no position to fly up to Alice so I just gave her a quick call every so often."

"Every day from what I hear."

"Well okay—most days while you were really sick. As for your washing, I just put a peg on my nose. I would have done it for anyone." She grinned at him cheekily. "Couldn't have you smelling like a desert rat, could we? The hospital staff wouldn't have wanted to come anywhere near you."

"Thanks Curly. You know how to make a man feel good about himself. I just wanted to let you know how much I appreciated everything you did for me."

"You didn't have to ask me out to dinner just to tell me that. You could have told me in the office today."

"Yeah sure, like that was the place to have a personal conversation. Anyway, this way I get to spend some time with you. I know I'm out of town a lot with the job, but when I'm here I'd really like to spend more time with you."

What did he mean? Chris saw her often.

Maria came back with their drinks, and asked for their food orders. Chris knew exactly what he wanted. Sarah hurriedly studied the menu. The selection was too big. Not pizza, she was definite on that. Maria stood there, pen poised and eyebrows raised. She had to choose something "Escalopes of Veal, thank you—with salad."

"Good choice." Maria took back the menus and went to greet new customers. Sarah wished she still had the card so she could hide behind it. She didn't know where this conversation was going, but an uncomfortable feeling in the pit of her stomach told her she might not like it.

"You already spend lots of time with me, Chris. There are the Friday night drinks and sometimes we have a barbecue round at the flats and everyone comes to those."

"That's right—me and a hundred others." The wry tone indicated his feelings. He resumed his fiddling, before shoving the cutlery aside and looking directly at her. "Those times are great Curly, but sometimes I'd like it to be just the two of us. I know you went through a terrible stretch after Dave died, but time's passing and he wouldn't expect you to remain on the sidelines forever."

Now he picked up the salt shaker, and started fiddling with that. "I don't want to rush you but I'm just putting it out there that I think you're a fantastic woman and I always have. I've kept a respectful distance but I've got the feeling in recent times you're ready to start moving on."

Was he going to reach across the table and try to take her hand? It was a distinct possibility. Sarah quickly moved her hands to her lap, hoping she wasn't too obvious. Looking at Chris properly for the first time in ages, she had to admit that for some woman, he would be a good catch. He hadn't fully recovered a healthy glow, but he would, and he had boyish charm and such an endearing smile.

As she mentally ticked off the attributes, she reminded herself he was kind, generous, funny and always a gentleman. She liked him—she really did. That was the catch. He was a great mate and she didn't want to do anything to spoil that. What to say? Where was the guide book when she needed one?

She sipped her wine, regarding him over the rim of her glass with affection. Chris had been a wonderful friend and support through the dark times since Dave's death. Both he and Mark had made it their business to call on her regularly, initially dragging her out when all she wanted to do was lie in bed with the blankets pulled over her head. They made sure she ate, even though she wasn't hungry. Gradually, they made her realise the sun still came up each day and reminded her she needed to embrace it.

He looked at her with an air of expectancy. Sarah needed to say something. She put her glass down, thoughts racing. "I probably haven't said it enough, but I appreciate everything you've done for me over the last year—Mark too of course." She paused. It was important to get this conversation right.

"There were some days when I couldn't see the point of anything anymore and you two didn't let me wallow. Nicely of course. It's thanks to you the pain surrounding Dave slowly eased. I'll never forget him, but I know I can't just live in the shadow of those memories either."

She glanced around at the other diners, still casting for the right words to explain how she was feeling. Everyone else was engaged in their own conversations, not paying her any attention. At least that was one advantage of sitting towards the back of the room. She turned back to Chris.

"You're right that the dark mood around me has lifted recently, and in part I have Joel to thank for that. When he came to town, he had no idea of my past and it allowed me to be a different person. With him, I wasn't Sarah, the woman whose fiancé had died—I was a woman he'd just met and who he wanted to get to know. At least I thought he did. He made me stop living in the past and start thinking about the future again."

She gave an involuntary sigh. It wasn't all positive. "Having said that, he also made me realise I'm still fragile and relationships require a lot of resilience. What I want more than anything is the support of good friends—friends like you and Mark and Kathy—you've been my rocks and I love you for it."

"Curly, I'll spare you the drama. I think I hear what you're saying here. You value our friendship and don't want to take it any further." There was a hint of resignation to these words.

"You can't blame a man for trying. Just to reassure you, we'll always be friends. Who else can tap dance on tables like you?"

Sarah threw back her head with a deep throaty laugh of relief. She should have known better than to think there was any threat to their friendship. She loved this man so much—it just wasn't in the way he wanted.

The stress of the day began to ease. Once again, it was Chris to the rescue. When it came, the meal was good. It could have been the company; it could have been the wine; or it could have been the fact they were snug inside while the heavens still poured outside. Once again, Chris had managed to push the right buttons to release her inner stress.

As they were paying their bill and leaving, new customers arriving announced that the river had finally started to run. The first surge had come through and no doubt it would get faster and higher through the night.

The rain had stopped, though the clouds ensured it remained an overcast night. A smell of damp earth permeated the night air and a chorus of insects indicated their pleasure at the unaccustomed moisture. Sarah thought she could hear some frogs.

"I love watching the river in flood," she said. "I've only seen it a few times in all the years I've lived here."

"If you're in no rush to get home, we can drive out through Heavitree Gap and have a look there. The road runs adjacent to the river at that point and we should have a good view."

"I'd like that. We can even watch it from the shelter of the car if it starts to rain again."

The Gap marked the entrance to the town through the MacDonnell Ranges. It was just wide enough to accommodate the river, the railway line and the road. Outside the Gap, a causeway led to the local farm area and provided the only local access to that region. Chris cruised slowly through the Gap towards the parking area, adjacent to the causeway.

They weren't the only ones who had come to have a look. The first rush of water had swept rubbish and debris in front of it and frothed up into a dirty foam as it encountered rocks, fallen trees and other large objects in its path. With the aid of street lighting, they could clearly see the swirling torrent. It already spread over the width of what was normally a wide meandering tract of sand, with sporadic water pools.

"Looks like a few other people have had the same idea," Sarah said.

A collection of vehicles stopped at the beginning of the causeway, while drivers assessed the flow and depth of the water. As they approached the crossing, the driver of an SUV started the engine and eased towards the edge of the water. There was a brief pause, and then, moving at a slow and steady pace, the vehicle started to cross.

"This is going to be interesting," said Chris. "I'm not sure I'd tackle this surge in a vehicle."

He pulled over to the edge of the road and they got out of the car to watch, drawn to the water's edge with the handful of onlookers.

"It's a heavy vehicle," said one. "It's only the start of the flood so he should be able to get across. Hope he doesn't want to come back the other way though. The water is rising fast."

"Yeah, but I don't think he really understood quite how fast," said another. "It's stronger than you think."

All eyes were fixed on the vehicle, moving slowly with a foaming wake fanning behind it. Water was building up against the side of it as the torrent encountered the large object. The vehicle slewed slightly with the force of the flow, and they could see now that the driver was fighting to retain directional control. Sarah held her breath. She was glad it wasn't her in the car. Then, a rush of water hit the rear panels and the back end of the car veered over the edge of the causeway.

The headlights pierced the sky at a crazy angle as the driver revved the engine, trying to regain traction. There was no hope of this happening. There was a collective groan as the front of the car also slewed around and slid off the causeway into the river, with the car floating erratically. The headlights highlighted the debris and turbulence, as it swung this way and that. The car settled deeper in the water, with the level halfway up the doors.

"Stupid bastard. He shouldn't have listened to her. I need a rope."

It was a familiar voice. *Mac*. Sarah turned and saw him standing at the water's edge, watching the disaster unfolding in front of them. Who shouldn't have listened to whom? With a sense of dread, she looked back to the vehicle again. Surely not.

"Mac—it's Sarah. Who's in the car?"

He turned and stared at her dazedly before recognition hit.

"Sarah—sorry I wasn't expecting to see you. It's Joel and Sophie. She was desperate to get home. She's got a host of animals on that property of hers and was worried that if she didn't get back there tonight they'd be cut off for days." He raked his hand through his hair distractedly. "If I can get a long length of rope, I can try to wade out there and tow them back in."

As they watched, the vehicle settled deeper into the water. It wasn't moving downstream anymore, so must have been snagged against something—perhaps a fallen tree trunk. The driver's window was wound down, and they could just make out a figure as Joel emerged and pulled himself up onto the roof of the car. He then leant down and extending his hand, helped Sophie up as well. The pack rack gave them something to hang onto, but the torrent buffeted the car, and their grip on the roof was tenuous.

"Don't be silly mate," commented another spectator to Mac. "You'd never get far in that torrent. There would be three of you drowned instead of only two. Best to wait for emergency services. Has anyone contacted them?"

Drowned? Sarah's heart missed a beat. "Chris, what can we do? We can't just sit here and watch while Joel and Sophie are washed off the roof."

Her thoughts went into overdrive. *Before long, the car will move from that position and then it could be over-turned or could sink in one of the rock pools. If they enter the water, they won't have a hope.* "Could we reach them with a truck, do you think? What about a fire truck with a long ladder?"

Another voice reported he'd rung the emergency hotline, but the crews were all out on previous calls. The spate of weather had brought with it a host of mini-disasters, and resources were already stretched to the limit. A crew would get there as soon as it could.

There was a silence as those watching digested this news. It was broken by the sound of Sophie's screams for help.

'Help us, somebody help us! Don't let us drown!"

"Sophie, it's Sarah! Hold on tight! We're not going to leave you. We're making a plan." She hoped that the wind hadn't carried her voice away. The horrible part was she had no idea what they could do. There wasn't any help coming, not for a while anyway.

Someone mentioned he had a life jacket in the car and others started talking about tying lengths of rope together. Perhaps—just perhaps—they could make a line long enough to reach them. There were a few crazy ideas thrown in the mix as well. All the while, more water was coming down the river and the level was rising.

190

"I'll get them." Chris raised his voice against the others. "Don't anyone do anything rash here. I'll drive out to the airport and get the NT Rescue Chopper. If I can get hold of a couple of crew members from the rescue team, one of them can be winched down to retrieve Joel and Sophie from the roof."

"But Chris—are you cleared for rescue work again? Visibility here is dreadful. If you get too close to the trees or the cliffs on either side of the Gap you won't stand a chance."

"If I don't try Curly, *they* won't stand a chance. There's no time to find anyone else. It's their only hope. By the time any other rescue gets here, they'll be long gone." He turned to Mac. "You work at the radio station—right? I'm heading out to the airport. I need to get hold of a couple of crew members but I have no idea where'll they'll be right now. Can you get a call put out over Radio Alice requesting them to get to the airport pronto? Hopefully, if they don't hear it, someone who knows them will and the message will get passed on. I gotta go. I need to get the chopper ready." He turned to Sarah. "I'll have to take the car. Perhaps someone can drop you back home. I might be a while."

"I'm staying right here. Be careful, Chris, and good luck. Hurry though."

His tail lights disappeared into the darkness as he drove off in the direction of the airport. Rain fell again in a steady drizzle, drawing a protest from the crowd. It was going to make a rescue even more difficult.

"Hold tight mate!" called Mac. "We're organising a chopper to lift you off. It might take a while. Don't go anywhere in the meantime."

You're so funny, Mac. "Chris is coming, Joel. He'll get you. Hold tight!" Sarah hoped he could hear her.

The scene was now illuminated by headlights from the cars that lined up along the river bank, facing the river. Sarah could just make out a thumbs-up gesture from Joel. He must have heard. Her heart contracted as she then saw Joel put his arm around Sophie. She clung to him with one hand, the other gripping the roof rack. Did they have more than a work relationship now? Sarah's eyes stung a little, and it wasn't from the impact of the rain.

Mac jumped into his own car and raced back to the radio station to put out the call Chris had requested. The radio station was just up the road and he could get the call out quickly. Sarah peered back along the road leading to the centre of town in the hope that emergency services were already on their way. There was no sign of them. For now, everything relied on Chris. All she could do was wait and pray. The driver of one of the parked cars had his car radio on turned up loud and they heard the call go out to the rescue chopper crew. It reassured them that something was happening.

Mac returned surprisingly quickly, sending up a spray of muddy water as he pulled up. He picked his way around puddles to re-join them. "I hit the phones and contacted one of the rescue crew members," he said. "He's on his way out to join Chris now. I left the announcer at the station in charge of putting out a broadcast and contacting others. I wanted to get back here in case there's anything else I can do."

"Thanks, Mac", said Sarah. "What you've done has already been a big help."

Shortly after, a car shot past them at speed in the direction of the airport. "Slow down, mate," muttered one spectator "or we'll have to rescue you too." There were some supportive comments but as one person said, given the circumstances he probably would've done the same.

"Shit," said Mac. "The water's much higher than when I left. This additional rain won't help. That roof-top must be so slippery."

The implications of this remark were met with silence. The danger of the situation was self-evident. A reporter from the station arrived and started doing interviews with those watching the drama unfold. Every so often, he would do a cross-over back to the station. A works vehicle turned up from the Alice Springs Council and workers in high visibility clothing erected barricades at the edge of the causeway, preventing anyone else from attempting the crossing.

Sarah regarded them with exasperation. *Pity you lot weren't here earlier. Surely, given the forecast this should have been done hours ago?* She knew it wasn't their fault though. There was more than one causeway over the river and probably they had been kept busy.

Joel should never have entered the water in the first place. Why didn't anyone stop him? She hunkered down into her coat, having turned the collar up as some protection against the rain. Her hair was a mass of wet ringlets and dripping from the ends and her shoes were starting to squelch.

"Sarah—get in the car." Mac beckoned her over to join him in the front of his Monaro while they waited. "No point in all of us getting drowned. You can't see any better from out there anyway."

It seemed wrong to be out of the rain while Joel and Sophie were in such a perilous situation, but she couldn't do anything that was helpful. Just wait.

Mac gripped the steering wheel, staring out at the river. "I told her she couldn't possibly drive her small beetle-like car over the river, and she got upset. Said she had to get home." He turned to face Sarah, the anguish showing on his face. "I went to the bathroom, and that's when Sophie asked Joel to drive her home. I didn't know until after they'd left. If I had, I would have stopped them. Being new to town, Joel wouldn't have understood the danger."

Mac hit the steering wheel in frustration. "He's a good bloke. Joel's made some positive changes at the station but e should've put his foot down. Sophie would lead anyone by the nose if she could."

There was nothing Sarah wanted to say to that. They sat there listening to the radio, but with a window down so they could also monitor what was happening outside. Their eyes didn't leave the two people clinging to the car roof. Water was now pouring in the open window Joel and Sophie had climbed through, and their prospects looked grim. Those watching from the river bank began talking about strategies for trying to reach them if Joel and Sophie were washed off the roof. Could they stay afloat? Was there a point where the river narrowed? Could they perhaps grab hold of a tree and climb that? None of it sounded feasible. It was empty talk. Sarah knew they were all trying to stay positive.

Suddenly, Mac turned down the radio. "Listen."

It was faint, very faint, but in the distance she could hear the chopper approaching. Peering in that direction, she could see not only the beacons attached to the aircraft, but also a powerful search light that was sweeping the river below. Jumping out of the car, she screamed above the ambient noise.

"Everyone, listen up. Here comes the chopper. If you have your car facing the river, put your headlights on now. If you have any spotlights, put those on too. The rescue team is going to need all the light they can get."

Everyone moved to comply and soon, bands of light were crossing the river. A few cars sat on the other side as well, attracted by the deluge, and they also turned on their lights. Sophie and Joel were caught in the web.

"Jeez, this is going to be hard. If Chris doesn't get it right, they'll all end up in the drink."

Mac said what everyone was thinking. The proximity of tall eucalypts and the adjacent cliffs made it a difficult retrieval. The noise as the chopper slowly manoeuvred to a position above the car enveloped those watching from below. The juddering of the chopper indicated Chris struggled to maintain the hover against the pummelling of the weather.

A crew member sat in the open doorway, his feet dangling over the edge as he peered at the scene below. He wore a life jacket over his standard issue overalls. The crew worked as a team, with each member contributing to the overall success of the rescue. If Chris misjudged his height, or the wind direction, or power requirements, it would not only be disastrous for Joel and Sophie but for the man trying to retrieve them.

All eyes on the ground strained upwards. The man stepped out onto the skid of the helicopter, and began his descent towards the raging river below. Sarah leant forward, gripping the dashboard for support as she peered at the unfolding drama. Another figure leant from the open door of the chopper.

"What's he doing up there? Mac asked.

"He's operating the winch," Sarah said. "He's also giving Chris directional instructions–higher, lower, to the right, etc. They practice this a lot."

The man on descent swung at the end of the cable. He was still some metres above the water but he wasn't close enough to the roof of the car. Communicating with hand signals to the winch operator, he slowly swung closer and lower. Joel stood up, balancing himself on the roof rack while Sophie clung onto his legs. In turn, Joel was able to grasp the legs of the descending man and draw him down onto the roof of the car.

The crowd maintained a heart-stopping silence during the descent, but now there were a couple of calls.

"He's down! That was bloody brilliant."

"You'll be right, Sophie. Hang in there!"

Sarah released the breath she'd been holding. Time was running out. The rescuer had carried down two additional life jackets with him, and the stranded pair quickly put them on.

He strapped Sophie into a harness and with the signal given to start winding, he and Sophie were winched up, leaving Joel to cling once again to the roof, this time on his own.

The chopper lurched alarmingly at one stage, causing the couple suspended below to swing and the crowd to gasp. After a moment, the winching started again and they moved slowly upwards until both could be dragged inside the cabin.

That left Joel. Water rose towards the top of the car, with debris building up against the side as it floated down river. The level climbed still higher. His tenure on the roof was limited. It could only be a matter of minutes. He was spread-eagled now, firmly gripping the rack as the car rocked.

"C'mon," urged Mac under his breath. "What's keeping you? Get back down there and grab him."

"They can only go so fast, Mac." Sarah was just as anxious but knew that safety of all concerned was paramount. "He'll be following procedures. They can't take risks." She was on Mac's side though. Shouldn't they be on their way back down again by now?

The crewman appeared at the doorway again, feet on the skid, looking down. He gave the signal and the lowering process began again.

The car swayed with the current. The wheels closest to the water flow were starting to lift and Joel was in greater peril than before. If the car rolled on its side, he could be trapped underneath. He wore the life jacket but that was no guarantee of survival. His predicament was obvious to everyone watching. The tension was palpable.

Sarah couldn't sit in the car any longer. The rain was blearing the windscreen. She jumped out, wanting to see more clearly. Tears prickled at the corners of her eyes, only then to slip over and blend with the rain on her cheeks. They slid a trickling path into the corners of her mouth as she muttered a prayer.

The man on the cable dropped lower. This time, Joel couldn't stand up to guide him to the car but he was able to reach up one hand to grasp the harness that his rescuer was holding. Some complex manoeuvring followed as Joel struggled to slip his feet into the harness and clip it tightly together. The crewman helped to steady him whilst this was happening and then deftly attached the cable to the harness. Signalling once more to the cabin crew, the cable tightened and the two men swayed gently as they were winched towards safety.

A cheer went up from the riverbank and a chorus of car horns sounded in celebration. As they watched, the two men reached the chopper and were dragged inside. The machine rose, orientated itself on track, and took off in the direction of the centre of town. Sarah guessed Chris would probably drop his passengers at the hospital where there was a helipad.

"Hey sister, I thought they were gone," Mac said punching her lightly on the shoulder in barely concealed elation. "He's one damn good pilot, that friend of yours. I reckon Joel owes him a beer."

Chapter 16

"THANK HEAVENS IT'S not about me this time. I didn't see the photographer. Not surprising I suppose, given the drama that was going on."

The Centralian Advocate lay on her desk, the article detailing every nail-biting moment. The photo showed Joel and his rescuer suspended by the cable, the roof of the car below them awash with flood waters. The rescue team got there in the nick of time. Looking at the paper, Sarah felt sick to the pit of her stomach. The total impact of the danger that Joel and Sophie had been in hadn't registered with the adrenalin of the moment. The photo exposed the full horror.

Several colleagues, coffee mugs in hand, had gathered in her office in search of every juicy detail. Of major interest was the role Chris had played, but after it had been thoroughly re-hashed and the finer details examined, they drifted off one by one, leaving Sarah to get on with her day.

She folded the paper, leaving the photo face down. How was Joel coping? He was probably fielding media enquiries for one thing and talking to the insurance company for another. *Are you still covered if you knowingly drive your vehicle through flood waters?* She wasn't sure and hoped she never had to find out.

The car hadn't been recovered. The flood waters would need to recede for that, but presumably it would be a write-off. She contemplated calling him, but then talked herself out of it. She'd had enough heartache. There was no point in courting any more grief. She had good friends around her and that was what she valued. Kathy though, in a subsequent phone call, had a suggestion for what she really needed.

"You've been down in the dumps for long enough. Time you booked yourself into *Hair About Alice*. It's the best remedy I know for lifting the pall of gloom and misery. Did you know they have vibrating massage chairs? Why don't you get some gold highlights? You should try something new."

Sarah smiled, holding the phone closer to her ear. "I'm not after anything too radical, but you're right. It is time I got this mop under control again. I'll see when they have a vacancy."

As Sarah did her run out to the airport during the afternoon, she saw the flood level in the river had dropped, but crossing the causeway was still not an option. Barriers on either side of the river ensured no other vehicle attempted it but there were plenty of sightseers. The opportunity to take photos of a river running through a desert town was an attraction. It happened so rarely.

Kids, their bikes propped against the bank, skipped stones in the water or threw in sticks and watched them float downstream. The water remained a disgusting muddy colour, and was choked with rubbish. Joel's car looked sad indeed. Water still lapped the bottom of the windows. At least the rain had cleared. The sky immediately above was ominous but there was hope on the distant horizon.

On her return to the office, a message on her desk indicated that Joel had rung and asked for Chris's phone number. Fair enough. Probably wanted to thank him. She gave the number to the office receptionist and asked the woman to call Joel and give him the details. She decided against returning the call herself. No point in embarrassing them both when it was Chris to whom Joel wanted to speak, not her.

Remembering Kathy's suggestion, she called *Hair About Alice*. The salon was open late that evening. They had a time slot free, so that was lucky. She could go there straight from work. With that arrangement in place, she settled down to the afternoon's tasks.

The appointment started with a hand-massage while she waited for her designated stylist to finish with the previous client. The young apprentice was earning her keep by providing the complimentary service to waiting clients. It was bliss. Sarah was tempted to throw off her shoes and proffer her feet for the same treatment. That would really release the tension. The stylist interrupted her reverie to invite her to take a chair, and ended that idea. The apprentice disappeared to the salon kitchen to make her a cup of tea while Sarah sat down in front of the all-revealing mirror.

"So, what are we doing today?" the stylist cooed as she ran her fingers though Sarah's hair, lifting locks for closer inspection. "Time for a makeover?"

"Why? Does it look that bad?"

"Not at all. I thought you might be looking for something a little daring."

"No, more of the same thank you. It just needs a tidy-up really and perhaps some highlights to make it interesting."

The stylist knew better than to push for anything too adventurous. Sarah was a long-standing client at the salon. Instead, she advised on potential colours for the highlights and disappeared to the rear of the salon to prepare the colouring potions. It gave Sarah a chance to eye off the magazines. The salon always kept the current issues. It made the visit more rewarding.

"Umm—Sarah?"

She looked at the woman in the chair next to her, draped in towels and a cape and sitting beneath a drying hood. She had to look twice before she realised who it was. Not someone she had expected or particularly wanted to see. *Sophie.*

"Oh—Sophie. I didn't know you came here." It was an inane comment but she was taken by surprise. She couldn't think of anything better on the spur of the moment.

"When you find a good cutter, you tend to stick with them. I've been coming here for years. I'm staying with a friend at the moment, but after last night I felt I needed some nurturing."

An uncomfortable silence followed. *I hope she's finished and out of here soon. I do not want to sit here making polite conversation for the next hour. Maybe I can bury myself in a magazine and she'll get the hint.* Sarah smiled politely and picked up the top magazine from the pile, hoping there was something in it worth reading.

"I want to thank you."

Sarah looked up into the green eyes that observed her intently.

"I know if it weren't for you and Chris, I probably wouldn't be here tonight. If we'd had to wait for emergency services to arrive, it would have been too late."

Sarah was embarrassed. "Look, I'm glad we came along when we did and we were able to help. It was all due to Chris really. If he hadn't thought to fire up the rescue chopper it might have been a different story but all I did was coordinate the lighting and pray! You had a great team batting for you in the air."

"Yes, I did, and I'm so grateful." Sophie paused a moment. "There's something I should tell you."

She paused again, this time meeting Sarah's eyes in the wall mirror, which somehow was less confronting.

"When we were lifted from the roof of the car, Joel insisted I was taken first. It was really dangerous by then, and

201

there was the risk that before they could return for him, he might be washed off the roof. If that were the case, his chances of survival were slim. We both knew that. It was a scary and emotional time."

Sophie paused, chewing her lip before continuing. "As the rescuer strapped me into the harness, Joel asked me to tell you something if he didn't make it."

Just the thought of that moment sent a wave of horror skidding over Sarah. The magazine slipped to the floor. She made no attempt to pick it up. She raised an eyebrow in mute query, a subtle gesture, which asked more than words.

"He asked me to tell you he was sorry."

"He was sorry?"

"Yes. He was sorry for what he said to you that day at the Regatta. He wished he could make it up to you."

"Why are you telling me this now?"

"Because I know that he was trying to ring you today and you didn't call him back. He was afraid you wouldn't."

"But what has this got to do with you?"

At this point, the apprentice arrived with the cup of tea. There was an uncomfortable silence while the girl carefully deposited the cup on the bench top, complete with a shortbread biscuit and obligingly picked up the magazine as well. When Sarah looked back at Sophie, the woman was still biting her lips as though chewing over a problem.

"Nothing, and yet in some ways, everything. If I hadn't persuaded Joel to drive me home, we would never have been in that situation. He wasn't to know how treacherous the river is in flood, or how deep it would be but I've lived here all my life. I don't have any such excuse. I should have known better but I thought we had enough time. I put us both at risk and for that I am truly sorry."

There was a catch to her voice and it was clear that she was becoming a little emotional. Sarah looked around and quickly grabbed a box of tissues from the shelf in front of them. She pushed it in Sophie's general direction. Sophie pulled out a tissue and dabbed at her face, resulting in smudges and panda eyes as she smeared her mascara. In exasperation, Sarah directed her to look at herself in the wall mirror.

"You'd better check your face."

While Sophie attended to the clean-up, Sarah sipped her tea and considered what she had heard. It didn't make a lot of sense. Sophie was feeling guilty, that much was clear but the situation had nothing to do with her. Could she slip into the magazine and avoid any further conversation? Surely the stylist would be back soon?

"The thing is," Sophie continued, smears reduced to faint shadows, "Joel really cares about you. He talks about you often. I admit I was sort of interested, but he's made it clear—nicely—that nothing's happening as far as we're concerned, and even I know that work relationships suck."

A slight voice tremor started in her voice and Sarah shoved the tissue box closer again. *Where was that stylist?*

"What I'm trying to say is I know Joel has had a lot on his mind lately. I put his phone calls through and I can't help learning a little about what's going on, and I know there've been a few challenges in your life—this is a small town after all, and well…" She gave Sarah a look of anguish. "…I did sort of say to Joel that day at the Regatta that I saw you fall over and that you were clearly intoxicated. It was an exaggeration. I'm sorry."

Exaggeration? Total fallacy more like. "But why? Why would you say such a thing?"

"Because I was stupid and I was jealous and you appeared to have everything going for you. When we were on that roof and I thought that maybe we weren't going to get off, a lot of things were running through my mind. I told Joel then I'd made a mistake. You'd stumbled on the uneven ground and reached out to someone else to steady yourself but you didn't fall at all, and you weren't drinking anything that I could see."

Sarah couldn't help noticing that even then, Sophie seemed to have fudged the truth, talking about witnessing a stumble rather than saying she had made the whole thing up. She felt sad and deflated rather than the need for retribution.

"And that was all you said about me at the Regatta—that I was intoxicated and falling over?"

"Well…" Sophie faltered and her voice dropped as did her eyes. "I did kind of infer you were ignoring Sam, but I didn't say that outright."

"And am I supposed to give you absolution now? Is that it? You've smeared my reputation but it's okay Sophie—all is forgiven. Is that what this is about—making you feel better?"

"No, you've got it all wrong. I just wanted you to know what happened, that it wasn't Joel's fault."

The stylist interrupted the conversation when she returned and swirled a plastic cape around Sarah's shoulders. Shortly after, someone else came over to check Sophie's hair was dry and to provide the final styling touches. Sophie rose from her chair, gathering her bag, and turned back to Sarah.

"I wanted you to know, that's all," she said in a voice that was barely above a whisper. Sarah nodded in acknowledgement, but refused to meet Sophie's eyes, not even in the mirror. There was nothing else she wanted to say.

Chapter 17

NIGHT HAD SET in by the time she walked through the door of her flat. She switched on the light and kicked off her shoes in one combined movement. It was good to be home. She needed to be in her own space to process what she'd just heard. That foot massage would have been good—if it'd been offered. The massage chair had been every bit as wonderful as Kathy promised, but relaxed was not what she was feeling right now. Angry, incredulous, disappointed—resigned even but not relaxed. Once again, forces outside of her control had intervened in her life and delivered a body blow.

"It's so unfair," she muttered to herself. "I must have been really bad in a past life. First Dave, now this."

On a rational level, she knew she was indulging in her own private pity party. After all, Dave was the one who'd died, not her, but all the same… Not one for drinking on her own normally, she took a bottle of Riesling from the fridge and opened it. Hang the consequences.

Glass in hand, she caught sight of herself in the hall mirror. Her hair was not totally tamed, but for once looked stylish and sophisticated in a tousled sort of way. The golden tips added an interesting effect and she wondered why she hadn't tried them before. Perhaps this would be the start of a new image. A pity this particular styling would only last until the next hair wash.

She peered more closely at the mirror, trying to see the sides and the back as well. They had shown her in the salon, but she had wanted to bolt for the security of home and hadn't paid attention. Looking at it now, she admitted to herself it looked good. She could drink to that at least. Maybe she even had some chocolate in the fridge. Vain hope, but no harm in looking.

The doorbell intruded on her reverie. She wasn't expecting anyone, but others from the complex often dropped by. Probably heard the fridge door and the clink of a glass. That lot could sense a drink a hundred yards away. It was an innate ability developed soon after arriving in Alice.

"It's okay—there is more than enough for two," she said, throwing open the door.

Joel stood there, bunch of roses in hand.

"Oh, it's you." She gaped in surprise, still holding her glass of wine. Just great. She didn't care what he thought.

"Are you expecting anyone? Am I intruding?"

"No, not at all. I thought it must be someone from one of the other flats."

"Is it all right then if I come in?" He sounded unsure of his welcome.

She hesitated. Why had he come? Why should she let him in?

Good manners won the day. "Yes, of course. Sorry, I don't usually keep people standing at the door."

She stood aside allowing him to enter. He halted inside the door and presented her with the flowers. "I remembered you liked roses."

She reached to take them. There was a small electric charge when her fingers touched his, which she chose to ignore. Smiling with a sweetness she didn't feel, she took the flowers and looked him full in the eye.

"Thank you, I'll find a vase. Would you like a drink? I've just opened a bottle."

Turning to find the vase and another glass gave Sarah the opportunity to gather her wits. She was acting cool and collected, but could feel her heart thumping. Instinctively, she reached up to twiddle the curl at the side of her face, belatedly realising it was no longer there.

"I like the new look. Suits you."

"Thank you." This time her smile was more genuine. "I've just come home from the salon." She turned to look at him. "I don't suppose you brought any chocolate with you?"

"Chocolate?" His confusion showed. "No—if I'd known you wanted it I would have picked some up on the way. I didn't think of it. How remiss of me."

Sarah placed the vase of roses in the middle of the table and stood back to admire them. Their subtle scent filled the room. That drink. She'd asked him about a drink. She poured a glass and put the bottle back in the fridge.

She handed Joel the wine, having assumed in the absence of advice to the contrary, that he was joining her. Too bad if he preferred something else.

"No need to stand—take a seat." She indicated one of the single-seaters and positioned herself at an end of the sofa, tucking one foot protectively underneath her in a defensive position. Leaning back against the armrest gave her a sense of control. Joel raised his glass in salute, accompanied by a slight nod that said, 'Here's to you'. *Here's to me, indeed. I think I look damn good.* It surprised her, but she was feeling remarkably in control.

Aloud, she said, "I'm glad last night ended happily for you and Sophie. It didn't look good for a while. Did the receptionist call you with Chris's details?"

"She did. I contacted Chris earlier. With all the dramas last night, and being whisked off to the hospital to check us both over, I didn't have time to thank him properly for coming and getting us. You have no idea what a relief it was when I heard you call out that he was on his way—second only to when he was hovering above. When I heard those rotors, I knew we had a chance and even more so knowing Chris was at the controls."

"I didn't think you were so enamoured of Chris."

"I've never doubted his abilities or professionalism for a minute. The questions I had last time I was here related to the depth of his feelings for you and vice versa. Blind Freddy could see he has an eye for you and I don't blame him. He wasn't alone in that regard."

Oh really? You weren't exactly open about your feelings, and other men aren't lining up at the door.

"I did tell you we were just good friends."

"So you did, and I'm glad that you and your good friend were on hand last night or the result might have been very different." He regarded her speculatively. "I had a chat to him today."

"Oh?" It was Sarah's turn to regard him.

"Yes, he said you and he are really good mates."

"Isn't that what I told you?" She took a sip of wine, to buy some thinking time. "Was that all?"

"It was a general discussion but that was the gist of it. Blokes aren't really into prolonged chatting. He mentioned your fiancé, and the devastation for you when he died."

She shifted uncomfortably in her seat. She still found it difficult talking about Dave, and discussing him with another man was especially so. Not so long ago it would have seemed tantamount to being unfaithful but suddenly it didn't feel like that anymore.

"I told you about Dave. He has been and always will be an important part of my life, and I don't want to forget him. I know I still have to keep living, and that's what I've been trying to do."

There was a moment's silence. "Chris sort of explained that. Amongst other things, he also assured me whatever designs he may have on you, he respects you too much to ever damage your friendship."

"I'm not sure I like the idea of you two discussing me. Why should you have to ask Chris about any of this when I'd already told you?"

"I didn't plan to talk to him about you. It sort of came up."

"Yes a few things seem to have 'sort of come up' today. By chance, I ran into Sophie at the hairdressers, and likewise had an interesting discussion, though not much of a prolonged chat either."

"Ah yes, Sophie. Persuasive young lady, that one."

"In more ways than one. She told me what she said to you at the Regatta—about me and my aberrant behaviour."

"She did indicate to me she may have been mistaken in what she reportedly saw. Sarah, I want to apologise to you. That's why I've come; also to explain a few things. I was under pressure that day and too quick to jump to conclusions. I took it out on you and that was grossly unfair."

"It seems Sophie wasn't the only one who was mistaken. I should have made sure Sam got back to you safely. I assumed in that enclosed environment, he wouldn't come to any harm walking back to the radio tent on his own. After all, he's not a little kid."

"No, he's not. I agree; I over-reacted and took it out on you. I am truly sorry for that."

"But what I really minded," she continued, "was the allegation that I habitually got drunk and fell over. I know the night we first met, I was in an exuberant mood, but drinking too much is not my usual style. I was embarrassed and humiliated in front of my friends."

"Now, I'm embarrassed, and rightly so. It was never my intention to do that. Even Sam told me off later that day."

"How is Sam"?

"He's fine—back with his mum in fact. I put him on a plane the next day, so yes, he's not such a little kid any more. I wanted to talk to you about Sam—amongst other things."

"Look, I've gathered since we first met that there are some family issues for you. Don't feel you have to tell me anything that's not my business."

"I need to and for several reasons. Firstly, it may help to understand my behaviour recently and secondly, I want to repair the damage I did to our relationship. The story doesn't just involve me, so I had to talk to someone else first to get consent to what I am about to tell you."

Sarah could feel a different sort of tension building inside her. She had no idea what she was going to hear, but she had the feeling that no matter what it was, the information would mean a significant change to them both. Did she really want to hear this? Was she ready for the consequences, whatever they might be?

"I might top up my wine and get a glass of water as well. Does your drink need freshening?" She was playing for time. "Don't stop. I'll just quickly put together some nibbles while you talk. I shouldn't be drinking on an empty stomach and probably neither should you."

"Don't go to any bother. I can wait until you're sitting again."

He rose and idly perused the books on her shelves, presumably wanting her full attention for whatever it was he wanted to tell her.

Sarah put together a platter of cheeses, olives, crackers and nuts—everything she could put her hands on quickly.

210

Placing it on the coffee table, she resumed her original position on the couch. Joel ceased his pacing and sat down again. He rolled his shoulders, and massaged his chin. It was a while before he spoke.

"You recall on the day we had the picnic at the Telegraph Station, I mentioned I had a sister—Carla."

"I'd forgotten her name, but yes you did mention a sister."

"Carla was the athletic one in the family. Her field was gymnastics and she was very good. She started from a young age and quickly became obsessed. She was determined to get to national standard and her goal was to represent Australia at international level, and in fact, that is what she did."

"Wait a minute—your sister isn't Carla Wainwright is she?" He nodded.

Why didn't he tell me this before? "I've seen her! I've watched her compete—on TV of course, but she was fantastic."

"Yes, that's Carla. She's earned her share of gold and silver and the family's really proud of her. She married her coach some time back and Sam is her son and as you know, my nephew."

"I'd wondered if you were going to tell me more about Sam."

"Yeah, well—it's a long story. Gymnastics is a gruelling sport and Carla got some significant injuries while she was competing. With her competitive spirit, she didn't want to slow down and relied heavily on pain killers to get her through. She was encouraged in this by Roger, her husband. He had a lot riding on her success, and attracted more funding and clients on the strength of it. He got some overseas contracts and established a strong reputation in the field as well. He really pushed Carla to keep going. She was his golden girl."

"I remember all the media attention. Weren't they a bit of an A-list couple?"

"Sure were. Anyway, with his overseas contacts, Roger got a range of pain relief drugs that weren't commonly available in Australia, the result being that Carla became dependent."

"She became addicted—is that what you're saying?"

He stood up again, and began to pace before halting in front of the window and looking out, his back to her. "Yep— my little sister became a drug addict. She was good at hiding it and the family had no idea. Her husband was complicit in concealing this from all concerned as well as being controlling. There came a point when everything started to unravel. She quit competitive gymnastics and started coaching as well. Sam was born during this period and from the outside, their life looked idyllic."

He turned back from the window. Sarah could see the anguish he was feeling as he told Carla's story. She couldn't imagine what life must have been like for a young woman who at one stage had enthralled the country.

"It was only later we found out what was happening. Carla's behaviour became more erratic and Roger began an affair with a younger gymnast—a teenager he was grooming for the next gold medal opportunity. It was like seeing him with Carla all over again."

Sarah took a handful of nuts, thinking about the impact on his sister. "She must have been devastated."

"She was, but I think by that time, she was over him and the relationship. I began to suspect there was emotional abuse behind the scenes and made sure she realised she was not alone. Any time she needed help, all she had to do was call me."

"That's what brothers are for. Carla's lucky you were watching out for her."

He sat down again, shaking his head. "She didn't call at first. When he finally left her for the younger replacement, she tried to cope on her own. The trouble was, her drug habit was expensive and Roger excluded her from his training college when he left. She had no income. She knew she needed to get off the drugs and tried to do it on her own. That was when she had a total breakdown and ended up in hospital."

"I don't think I heard anything about this."

"You wouldn't have. I became skilled at keeping the media at bay and controlling what information leaked into the public arena. I found a private clinic for Carla and the family rallied around to help fund it." He pulled a face. "Actually, that's what she thinks. I had a private word with Roger and the threat of what some adverse publicity could do to his career was instrumental in getting him to cough up. It was only what she was due, anyway."

"He sounds a total pig."

"There's not much favourable I could say about him, except of course that Sam was the result of the relationship. He's a good kid and fortunately nothing like his father."

"Judging by his swimming activities, he's taking after his mother."

"Perhaps, but it's too early to make any real call on that. By nature he takes after his mother and for that I'm relieved."

Arresting though this story was, Sarah still wondered why Joel was telling her all this. It was a day for unexpected revelations. She untucked her feet and stretched out along the couch, not feeling as defensive as she had earlier. *Poor Sam. He must have grown up in a challenging environment.*

"Does Sam see anything of his father now?"

"Occasionally. I would never deny Sam the right to have that contact. It's up to him to form his own opinions of the man. Carla has always been very careful not to bad-mouth Roger in Sam's hearing."

Looking at the platter of nibbles, Sarah realised she had absentmindedly been eating all the nuts. She proffered the platter to Joel. "Don't let me eat all of this. Carla sounds like a respectful parent, in spite of what was going on in her life."

Joel gave a resigned shrug, acknowledging her remarks. "The last few years have been difficult for her and she's still emotionally fragile. At times, she suffers enormously with depression and I've arranged for an international student to board with her and Sam. In return for cheap accommodation, Miguel keeps an eye on the household, makes sure Sam gets to school if Carla is in the grip of the black dog again, and keeps me posted if there are any dramas."

Ahh—so that's who Miguel is. I'm so glad I never said anything about him. Aloud, she said, "That sounds like a practical solution; good for Sam to have another male around the house too."

He picked up some cheese and biscuits before rising again and resuming his stance by the window. Sarah hadn't seen him in this state before. Footsteps sounded on the driveway outside. She hoped it wasn't anyone else coming to visit. The timing would be abysmal. The crunching sound faded and wiping some crumbs from around his mouth, Joel continued.

"One of my concerns with taking this job in Alice was ensuring Carla was coping and that Miguel was confident as well. I had to slip back a couple of times to check everything was running smoothly."

"And so there was a problem recently?"

He sighed. "You could say that. Carla had been prescribed a new anti-depressant and it had a weird effect on her. She stopped eating, stopped sleeping and her behaviour became quite erratic. It got to the point where Miguel couldn't cope. He's been so helpful but he's only a student after all. He rang me the night that I had dinner here to let me know what was going on. The news stressed me, and that was when I had to leave so abruptly."

"Well at least I know now it was nothing I'd done."

"You didn't really think that, did you? I could kick myself. I'm sorry—I didn't mean that to happen. I had to go back to Melbourne and get Carla re-admitted to a clinic for a period, getting her medication reviewed and her condition stabilised."

He was quiet for a moment, and Sarah waited, knowing there was more to come. He pulled a face, and briefly rubbed the side of his face before speaking again.

"I decided to bring Sam back with me, for the duration. I wouldn't expect Miguel to look after him over that time, and our parents were off on the annual caravanning trip. It seemed the best solution."

"You know, I would have understood if you'd told me this before. You could have confided in me."

"I wanted to at times, I really did. Carla had made me promise I wouldn't tell a soul about her situation and I had to abide by that. She's desperate to prevent the story about her addiction and her state of mind getting into the public arena. She was totally drug free while she was competing, but you know how it is. All it takes is for there to be a hint of scandal or wrong-doing for a reputation to crumble." He gestured with his free hand, the other clutching his wine. His expression was earnest, beseeching almost.

"Her standing in the gymnastic community means a lot to her. Her only source of income is coaching and she would be barred from that if there was any hint of doping.

"You're right, I'm sure. I can hear the public outcry now."

"Also…" his explanation morphed into a sneer, "…the lovely Roger has threatened to take legal action, claiming full custody over Sam. We don't want him to find out about the breakdowns or the clinic visits. It would give him ammunition in claiming Carla is an unfit mother. That's why I flew off the handle when Sam disappeared. It was an over-reaction, I know, but I didn't want to think I'd added to the problem."

"What an awful man. I can understand where she's coming from." Nibbling a slice of cheese, Sarah frowned pensively. "So why are you telling me this now? What's changed?"

"Carla knows about you. I've mentioned you a few times and I gather from our phone conversations that Sam has told her about you as well."

"I'm not sure what Sam has reported will have necessarily been good. He appeared to be either bored or embarrassed around me, and he probably thinks I fall over drunk all the time!"

"Never assume what a twelve-year-old boy is thinking. It's got me into strife numerous times. However, I have it on good authority he thinks you're all right, and given the way he chewed my ear off after the Regatta, he doesn't think you're a hopeless drunk."

It was reassuring to know that Sam at least was in her camp. If she ever saw him again, she would be especially nice to him, even if he was mono-syllabic.

Joel finally stopped his pacing, and sat down next to her on the couch this time, leaning forward and looking directly at her. It raised a sense of anticipation. The butterflies in Sarah's stomach were in combat and trying to escape. *Thank God I already have a drink. Otherwise, I'd be looking for one.*

Joel reached for his drink as well. Perhaps he was feeling the same. "By this stage, I knew what Sophie had told me while we were in the river. She'd lied about you being drunk and neglecting Sam and I didn't sleep much last night. Adrenalin was pumping and I had a lot turning over in my mind; in particular, you."

"Me? Why me in particular?"

"Do you really need to ask?"

"Yes, I think I do."

"I knew I had to repair the damage I'd done to our relationship and I knew I wanted it to be a whole lot more. I had to explain to you everything that was going on in my life and to do that I had to get Carla's understanding and permission. When I rang her today, I explained to her how I felt about you and asked if I could tell you about her."

His gesture was one of open-handed appeal.

"Also, after my little adventure last night, I had to call her and explain what happened. I knew she would find out with the media coverage and the last thing I wanted was cause her increased anxiety."

"So let me get this clear. You told your sister how you were feeling about me before you told me?"

"Why have I got the feeling I'm on a hiding to nothing? Sarah…" He stopped and took a breath. "Discussing my feelings with you is important and that's what I'm trying to do, but I wanted to tell you everything and for that I had to explain to Carla why it was necessary. When I was clutching that damn roof last night, watching the water steadily rise and feeling the car shifting position with the force of the water, I honestly thought for a while we wouldn't be saved."

"You're not alone there. Watching from the bank was frightening enough. I was so scared the evening was going to end differently to what it did. It must have been one of those 'life flashing before your eyes' moments." She offered a weak smile.

Joel nodded. "I was sad—really sad. You and I had unfinished business and I desperately wanted to do something about it. Even before Sophie made her little admission, I had decided I was going to make things up to you, and then it seemed I wouldn't have the chance." He closed his eyes briefly before looking at her in appeal. "Do you think I could have another drink? I've just about talked myself hoarse here."

"God I'm so sorry. I was so engrossed with what you were saying that I totally forgot my manners."

Sarah jumped up and fetched the bottle from the fridge. When she brought it over to fill up his glass though, he stood up. Taking the bottle from her, he put it down on the coffee table. Puzzled, she looked up at him. Didn't he want a top-up after all? He reached out and grasping her arm, drew her close to him. She noted again how tall he was. Her breath quickened, and her heart gave a little jump as he wrapped his arms around her.

"It's so long since I've held you close. Did I tell you what I feel for you?"

"No," she whispered. "All you've done is talk about it but you still haven't told me anything of real substance."

"Sometimes, actions speak louder than words." One hand slid slowly down to the small of her back, drawing her close to him, while the other tangled itself in her hair, bringing her lips within kissable distance. Her eyes were fixed on his lips, drawing closer. The anticipation was delicious, but not as much as when his mouth finally claimed hers.

There wasn't any resistance, and the kiss that he gave was exploratory, tantalising and then passionate.

"I'm getting some understanding about what you're trying to say," she said. "Tell me again in case I got it wrong."

He was more than happy to oblige, before pulling back and looking down into her eyes. "I wanted to tell you Sarah Hartford that since the first night I met you I thought you were the craziest woman I knew. When I saw you emerge from your bedroom the following morning, I thought you were the most tantalising woman I knew. As I got to know you better, I realised you were the funniest, kindest, most intelligent and sexiest woman I knew. All of that adds up to a pretty fantastic package and what I'm saying, is I don't want to spend any more time apart from you than I can possibly help— and I really like your hair."

"What do you mean 'when you saw me emerge from my bedroom'? You were asleep!"

"Well I thought I was dreaming at first. This tousle-haired Venus emerged through that door and I was utterly smitten."

She blushed a flaming red. "You didn't say anything! You didn't let me know you were awake!"

"By the time I realised what was happening, I thought it prudent to pretend I was still asleep. I'd be lying if I didn't say that you created a lasting impression. Of course, my memory might be fooling me. Do you think—*kiss*—if I asked nicely—*kiss*—we might refresh my memory sometime soon?"

Sarah looked up into those mesmerising eyes, trying to make sense of the myriad of thoughts that raced through her head. As a day of surprises, it rated highly. Her gaze slid to those kissable lips, now smiling in what could be amusement—or invitation. Perhaps both. There was something appealing about a man with a sense of humour. Dave had that. What would he think now? Would he approve? She thought of Joel's protection of his sister, and concern for Sam. That ticked many boxes.

Her thoughts flicked to the future and the level of commitment she could give. Recent weeks had been such a roller coaster. They had challenged her emotions and readiness to love again. She would always have a place in her heart for Dave, but she had a future as well. Could she trust her heart? Was she ready for this relationship? His arms tightened around her. She wanted him to kiss her again.

A slight elevation of an expressive eyebrow indicated Joel was waiting for her response. Her heart quickened at the thought of what he was suggesting. *Yes, oh yes please!*

"Mm—that might just be possible. What are you like at foot massages?"

"I've not previously had a foot fetish, but I am sure with some direction, I could work on that, toe by delicate toe. Tell me how you like it. Which foot first?"

"If there's one thing I like, it's a quick learner. Let me slip my shoes off. I might need to lie down for this."

"Absolutely. You need to take the weight off your feet. Allow me." With seemingly minimal effort, he picked her up and pushed open her bedroom door.

Chapter 18

MURMERS AND RUSTLES in the crowd indicated both anticipation and impatience. Alex, arms folded, gave the appearance of wanting the whole thing to be over rather than just beginning. Kathy tucked her arm through his.

"I really appreciate you coming with me, sweetheart," she said. "Sarah was surprised when I told her you would be here, but I think she was pleased."

"Astonished would have been more like it," he replied. "I still can't believe you talked me into this."

"It's because you love me, and we both want to support Sarah. She's been such a good friend." She smiled at him with the assurance of someone who knows she is unquestionably right. "Anyway…" she continued in a low voice, "it gives you a chance to get to know Joel better."

She turned to the man on her other side. "It's already five minutes past. They must be about to start."

He gave her a brief smile, punctuated with a nod.

On cue, guitar music filled the auditorium. It began suggestively, like the beginning of a story, drawing the listeners in before picking up pace and rhythm. The curtains glided open to reveal a darkened stage, and a single spotlight on a musician playing a guitar.

There was a stamping of feet and a second spotlight picked up the figure of a woman as she spun in from the wings. Her ruffled skirt flared wide before wrapping around her legs when she came to a halt in the centre of the stage. More rhythmic stamping followed, and a spotlight highlighted the figure of a man as he danced in from the opposite wings, and joined the woman in the centre. The music paused; in a moment of intense silence, the couple stared at each other. The man reached out to seize his partner's waist, and the musician sprang into life, leading the couple on a flamboyant dance that left the audience applauding and the dancers' breasts heaving.

A troupe of dancers followed, their skirts billowing in a kaleidoscope of colours as they twirled and stamped their way through the program.

"They're good, aren't they?" she said, nudging her husband in the ribs.

"Not bad—for that sort of thing. I couldn't see Sarah. Was she in that mob?"

Kathy knew this praise was as effusive as Alex was likely to get. "She was. I'll point her out when she comes on next. She was the one in deep purple and black."

Alex gave a grunt of acknowledgement.

Kathy turned to Joel. "Did you see her? What did you think?"

"It took me a few seconds, but yes, I saw her. It helped that I witnessed some of the hysterical preparations for tonight. I don't know who was more stressed in the end—her or me! You've no idea the number of foot massages it took to get her this far."

Kathy's eyebrows rose, but she didn't press for more information. The next item was about to start and she focussed on the stage instead. When the curtains parted, a couple were already centre stage. The guitarist strummed an opening chord and the dancers each flung one hand in the air, the other clasping their partner's waist.

"That's Sarah!" Kathy hissed excitedly. "This is her solo event."

"She didn't tell me about this," Joel muttered. "I can see why—she's dancing with Tomás." He raised his voice. "Unhand her, you devil."

"Shhh!" A woman in front of them turned around and glared. Kathy suppressed a giggle, while Joel pulled a face at the back of the woman's head.

The dance was truly mesmerising, even if you didn't know the couple on stage. Kathy was impressed as she noted the confidence with which her friend interacted with Tomás and responded to the music. Taking those classes was the best thing Sarah could have done. As the dance ended, Kathy leapt to her feet, clapping and cheering.

"Bravo! Bravo!"

An ear-piercing whistle beside her made her blink in surprise. Joel stood with his fingers in his mouth and gave a loud whistle of appreciation that ricocheted around the auditorium. The woman in front swivelled around with her hands over her ears. Joel sat down again and directed a smile at her, which said it all. *Lady, if you don't like me whistling at my girl, tough titties.*

By the time Sarah arrived in the foyer area after the final curtain, most of the crowd had left. She had changed out of her costume, but her hair was still in a sleek roll at the back of her head, and secured with a clip of flowers. Her face split with a wide grin of excitement as she raised it for Joel's kiss.

"What did you think? Was I good or not?"

"Careful, mate," Alex muttered. "There's only one answer to a question like that."

"Good? You were fabulous. I was so impressed." Joel didn't need prompting. His enthusiasm was genuine. "It's worthy of a celebration. Just as well I've reserved the best table at Martine's, and told them to put the champagne on ice."

Kathy offered her congratulations, and even Alex said she had put on a spectacular display, "just like a real dancer."

"Thank you, Alex," she said. "I'll take that as a supportive comment."

"If we want the restaurant to keep that table for us, we should be going," said Joel. "They were emphatic about being on time when I booked."

"Great," Sarah said. "With all the excitement in the lead up to tonight, I hardly ate a thing. Now, I'm starving. I could eat a horse, or at least a small palomino."

The restaurant was bustling by the time they arrived. Sarah was still on a high, regaling them all with tales of what had gone on behind the scenes and what a thrill it had been to dance with Tomás. Joel rolled his eyes, but refrained from comment.

"So, are you continuing with classes?" Kathy asked. "Who knows where it could take you."

"I don't think so. I'll stick to dancing on table tops, though I'll probably continue the Spanish lessons. I'd like to visit Spain one day, and Spanish is spoken in many other countries."

"Can I suggest," said Alex dryly "that this is not an appropriate table top for dancing on?"

"Alex, you're no fun at all. Give me some more champagne, and I might be tempted."

The waiter stopped by their table and topped up their glasses, draining the last of the wine. "Another bottle?"

There was a moment of frozen silence, as three pairs of eyes sought each other. Sarah broke into giggles. "I was only joking. Of course, we'll have another bottle." After surveying the table in some confusion, and getting a brief nod from Joel, the waiter hurried off, returning a short time later with the new bottle.

Sarah couldn't remember when she had last felt this happy. It was wonderful to see Kathy and Alex, but Joel's support meant so much. Initially, she tried to keep the concert quiet, scared she would make a fool of herself. Kathy had a way of finding out things, and then the Community College promoted the night through a public announcement at the radio station, so Joel found out as well.

"What's this I hear about a concert featuring flamenco dancing? Does that involve your class? Are you a part of that?" He waited until a lazy Sunday morning lie-in at her apartment, when she was in no state to come up with a plausible denial.

"Ye-e-es, my class is involved, but it's nothing special."

"So do I have to book a ticket or can I pay at the door?"

"Joel, you can't go! I'll be so embarrassed. My dancing's not for public consumption."

"Why not? It was before."

She didn't stand a chance. By the time Joel and Kathy joined forces, it turned into a major outing, with Alex as well. Now she was glad it had. Her solo had been a great success and dining with Joel and her friends was a great way to mark the occasion.

"I'm so glad now you could all come. The idea terrified me at first, but it was only nerves getting to me. I'm so self-conscious in social situations."

Kathy raised one eyebrow with an ironic smirk. "Sarah, I remember when I first arrived in Alice. You over-awed me with your chutzpah, and ability to manage any social situation. You still do, as a matter of fact."

"I get by, but I can only do that with having such good friends around me." She beamed earnestly at them all. Under the table, Joel's hand sought hers, reminding her here was one person in particular who had come to mean so much.

"It was a great night, wasn't it?" she remarked as she brushed out her hair on their return to her apartment. As often happened, Joel was spending the night with her. "You and Alex seem to be getting on as well."

"We're not bosom buddies by any means, but we can hold down a reasonable conversation. It takes a while to break down his natural reserve."

"I know what you mean. You've no idea the dramas he and Kathy went through when they first met."

Joel came up behind her, and reaching around her waist, nuzzled into the back of her neck. "Sarah, this may surprise you, but right now I have no interest in talking about either Kathy or Alex, good friends though they may be." He'd partially undressed, and she was conscious of his bare torso pressing against her.

"Have I told you lately how good you smell?" he asked.

"I'm sure you have, but I'm happy for you to tell me again. Why stop at once?"

He massaged the back of her shoulders, and she gave a small moan of ecstasy, leaning back into him. "On second thoughts, no need to talk, just keep doing what you're doing."

"It works better if you get out of these clothes. Easier still if you're lying down."

"Is that so?" Throwing the brush down on the dressing table, she swivelled around within his grasp so she could face him. Her actions were slow and deliberate, as she drew his head down to meet hers with one hand, and ran her fingers over his bare chest with the other. That was all it took. With a low growl, he wrenched her blouse over her head, and fumbled with the catch of her skirt.

She stood there a moment, a slight smile creasing the corners of her mouth. "Allow me," she said, pushing him back a step. Maintaining eye contact, she stepped out of her skirt, casting it to a corner of the room. She then slipped off her bra, and flung it in the direction of the skirt. That just left her panties. Head on one side, she lowered her eyes seductively, before raising them again to meet his. She kicked the panties to the same corner of the room, and stood before him in glorious nakedness. A corkscrew curl slid over the side of her face in a statement of its own.

She struck a pose and with one hand on her hip, flung the other in the air. "Olé."

"Sarah, you are the most fabulous, funny woman I've ever met. Have I told you how much I love you?" Scooping her up, Joel took the few steps to the bed before flinging her onto it, followed by himself.

Her eyes welled with tears. "No, you haven't. I'd remember that. You can tell me as much as you like."

"You're crying. Sarah, don't cry. What have I done?"

"You beautiful man, you've filled a hole in my heart, that's what you've done. I'm not crying—I'm happy. Tell me again," she demanded "Tell me properly."

Raising himself on one elbow, so he could look into her eyes, Joel trailed a finger from the corner of her mouth, down her throat and circled the breast that quivered beneath his hand. "Sarah, from the tips of your toes, to the curls on your head, I love every bit of you. I love your generosity of spirit; I love your sense of humour, and most of all, I love you. I love the fact you've let me into your life."

"Joel, you've given me so much. It might not have been obvious, but I was not in a good place when you arrived. I was still grieving and I had lost my trust in so many aspects of life." She reached down to seize the hand still making its gentle journey of exploration, so that she knew she had his full attention.

"Have I told you how much I love you?"

This time, he was the one who blinked with emotion. "No, you haven't, but you can tell me as much as you like."

Australia

The Red Heart is set in Alice Springs, which is in the centre of Australia and the southern-most city of the Northern Territory. Kathy's family lives in Adelaide, the capital city of South Australia.

I'd love to hear your thoughts after reading *Trust Your Heart*. There are several ways you can do that:

- emailing me at <u>emily@emilyhussey.com.au</u>
- leaving a review online at place of purchase.

Your comments will help me in providing a great story, and your reviews will be helpful to future readers.

Don't miss out on your free download!

If you enjoyed this book, you might like to read a collection of short stories in

Romance in the Stone

To receive your *free* copy, click HERE or

copy and paste https://bit.ly/2LFsLmS into your browser.

THE RED CENTRE SERIES

The Red Centre Series is set in and around Alice Springs, in the centre of Australia and also known as the Red Centre. Meet all the central characters in the prequel, **Journey to the Heart**.

The Red Heart

Kathy Sullivan is excited about taking up her new job as a pilot in Alice Springs. She was surprised at the antagonism directed towards her by Alex Woodleigh, owner of Mulga Downs. She knew that it could be hot in the Red Centre, but Kathy had no idea how much heat she would generate. In the sky, she was in full command, but back on the ground she was in danger of losing her cool. Emotions peak when disaster strikes during a remote flight, forcing them to acknowledge the underlying cause of their conflict and antagonism.

Trust Your Heart

Embracing liquid refreshments a little more exuberantly than usual, Sarah falls off a table and into Joel's life. She introduces him to life in and around Alice Springs, but secrecy, for whatever reasons, gives rise to more problems than it hides. As water rises around him in the flooding Todd River, Joel is forced to question who he trusts. Is it too late for him to convince Sarah that with him, she has a chance for renewed happiness?

Follow Your Heart

Tragic events in her formative years colour Melissa's perceptions of her place in the world. Trust and commitment are not concepts she embraces. In a journey that takes her from a remote Australian station, to the high fashion world of

Sydney and beyond, Melissa learns valuable lessons. She realises that family can be broader than you appreciate, and that she has choices to make in who she lets into her life, and who she loves.

Emily Hussey

Emily Hussey resides in a coastal suburb of Adelaide, South Australia. She has lived in several Australian cities, and spent a few years living in Alice Springs, the setting for the Red Centre series.

While there, she also obtained her private pilot's licence, providing the technical background for Kathy Sullivan's flying exploits in her first book, The Red Heart. Although all of the characters in these stories are fictional, facets are recognisable in many of the people who still live there today.

She enjoys the short story format, and has been published in local anthologies. Those stories are in varied genres, getting to know people and the world as seen through their eyes.

Website: http://emilyhussey.com.au,
Queries: http://emilyhussey.com.au/contact/.
Facebook: https://www.facebook.com/EmilyHusseyAuthor/
Goodreads Page: https://www.goodreads.com/Emily_Hussey
Email: emily@emilyhussey.com.au